Kiss a Rake at Midnight

Chronicles of the Westbrook Brides

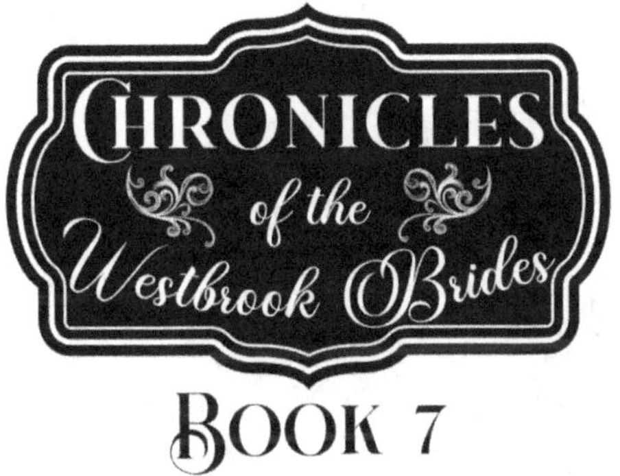

Book 7

USA Today Bestselling Author

Collette Cameron®

SWEET-TO-SPICY TIMELESS ROMANCE®

Blue Rose Romance® LLC

"Why are you looking at me like that?" she asked.

"Because, I am again reminded what an extraordinary woman you are."

Attn: Permissions Coordinator

Blue Rose Romance® LLC

PO Box 167

Scappoose, Oregon 97056 USA

collettecameron.com

eBook ISBN: 978-1-955259-69-9

Print Book ISBN: 978-1-955259-79-8

PRAISE FOR...

See What Readers Are Saying About
Kiss a Rake at Midnight!

★★★★★ "There were a few twists and turns that had me on the edge of my chair. I couldn't put this story down. Well done!"

— IREAD

★★★★★ "A lovely novella – the chemistry between Fletcher & Siobhan sizzles plus there's danger & mystery – I loved it!"

— JANET

★★★★★ "I found myself instantly wrapped up in the emotion and excitement of this tale, and just could not put it down. Loved it!"

— JAYNE BUTCHER

★★★★★ "This was a quick-moving story with adventure, intrigue, great characters, a shocking plot twist, and a heck of a love story."

— KRISTI HUDECEK ASHWILL

★★★★★ "Great read with some intrigue, mystery with lots of passion and love too."

— NANNA

KISS A RAKE AT MIDNIGHT

A ROMANTIC OPPOSITES ATTRACT MYSTERY & SUSPENSE FAMILY SAGA REGENCY ROMANCE

CHRONICLES OF THE WESTBROOK BRIDES
BOOK SEVEN

COLLETTE CAMERON®

GET YOUR FREE BOOK!

THE REGENCY ROSE®

JOIN MY EXCLUSIVE MAILING LIST
AND GET A FREE EBOOK!

Plus Sneak Peeks, Giveaways, Contests,
Exclusive Content and More...
P.S. I promise only good stuff ~ no spammy stuff!

Scan the following QR Code to join
The Regency Rose VIP Group Mailing List
and get your FREE BOOK!

Thank you,
Collette Cameron®

THE REGENCY ROSE®

VIP CLUB

AUTHOR'S NOTE

I love to use memorable names to reflect the memorable personalities of my characters. Siobhan, is the name of my heroine in *Kiss a Rake at Midnight.* It's a lovely name, don't you think?

The name Siobhan is of Irish origin and is pronounced **"shuh-VAWN."** It is derived from the Irish name "Síobhán," which is a variant of the name "Joan" or "Jeanne." Siobhan is often interpreted to mean "God is gracious" or "gift of God." It is a popular name in Ireland and among people of Irish descent.

I hope you enjoy getting to know Siobhan and Fletcher.

Happy Reading,
Collette Cameron®

ONE

De la Chance Social Club
London, England

JULY 1827 – EARLY MORNING

As was Fletcher Westbrook's wont, he walked through his social club's now silent and empty rooms with a cup of strong coffee. Tonight, like every other night, the place would teem with glittering guests eager and, in some cases, desperate for a few hours of entertainment.

Caution and wariness tempered the sense of pride that accompanied these daily inspections. Someone had slipped a threatening note beneath his office door last night.

The first such secret message in months.

"Bloody, sodding hell."

Fletcher swore beneath his breath before blowing on the scalding, sweetened brew and taking a bracing gulp. Nothing suspicious had occurred since last March when Torrian Westbrook, his cousin and a private detective, had apprehended the offender responsible for setting two fires, as well as sabotaging and vandalizing Fletcher's enterprises and sending other ominous letters.

The culprit, Mike Prescott, a low-end gaming hell competitor, hadn't appreciated Fletcher's scruples or losing elite customers to the classier, and quite frankly safer, establishment. Prescott had grown careless, hence his apprehension and imprisonment.

As Fletcher stood in the card room with its dozens of round tables, black Italian marble fireplace, and the occasional cobalt blue and gold striped damask settee, he pondered this unwelcome and unfortunate turn of events. He honestly believed he'd put that troublesome annoyance behind him for good.

Until last night.

His half-brother, Leonidas, and the only Westbrook besides Fletcher and their cousin Torrian Westbrook, who knew the whole situation, believed the harassment was over too. So much so the deliriously happy scoundrel had married Fletcher's new Scottish bookkeeper and currently enjoyed a honeymoon in the South of France.

Perhaps Fletcher had grown lax—let his guard down too soon.

But why shouldn't he have done?

Convicted of attempted murder, arson, and a half dozen other crimes, Prescott rotted away in Newgate.

One thing was for certain.

He couldn't be behind this latest episode.

So, who was?

Perchance, Prescott hadn't acted alone as he vowed, and his accomplice had become emboldened once more.

Mouth tight, Fletcher searched his memory for unfamiliar faces when he'd made his final surveillance of the club last evening, just before midnight. The mental inventory did little good. New club members were as numerous and common as pigeons in London.

What set *De la Chance* and his other establishments, *Ivories & Aces* and *The Emporium Theater,* apart from other gaming dens and men's clubs was Fletcher's strict, unrelenting vetting of members as well as absolute intolerance for known cheats, rakehells—*present company excluded, of course*—and randy men on the prowl making overtures toward Fletcher's female employees.

He employed over twenty of the best bodyguards in London to ensure the women remained unharried and the premises were as impenetrable as a cloistered virgin nun behind convent walls. Yet, somehow, someone had managed to not only sneak onto the grounds, but they'd found their way undetected to the private quarters on the club's other side.

Unlike many gaming hells, his upper rooms weren't available for liaisons with bit o' muslins on his payroll. Fletcher never had and never would employ prostitutes.

It must've been a guest who breached his inner sanctum.

But who?

Why hadn't one of his security team seen them?

Fletcher's nape hair stood on end, alerting him that he wasn't alone.

Slowly, he rotated toward the card room's entrance, prepared to defend himself with the ugly knife sheathed at his waist. Upon recognizing the small form sauntering through the opening, adorned on either side with heavy royal blue draperies held in place by a thick gold silk cord, he blew out a relieved breath.

Sean Kenney, a perpetually cheerful, if somewhat small and frail Irish lad of all work, gazed around the room with the chairs overturned on the tables that he was tasked with returning to the floor each morning. Unlike most of the club's other employees, Sean and a few others who tended to more menial tasks weren't required to wear all black.

Today, his delicate features wan, the lad seemed tense and distracted.

Nevertheless, he touched two slender fingers to his ever-present flat tweed cap.

"Good morning, sir. Howya today?"

"I am well." Physically, yes. But unrelenting worry niggled in the back of Fletcher's mind. He must find the culprit before things became dangerous once more. He took another sip of coffee. "Yourself?"

He'd learned long ago that when he took a genuine interest in his personnel, not only did they work harder, but Fletcher could, with a great deal of accuracy, determine which of them would become loyal, long-term help. Consistency among his employees proved essential to keeping his establishments running smoothly.

What he couldn't determine at this moment, however, was Sean's age, though if Fletcher hazarded a guess, he'd suppose the lad was in his late teens. Perchance sixteen or seventeen.

Small for his age, likely due to malnutrition, the youth often conducted himself and spoke like someone older and more mature. His eyes often held a world-weary glint, and fine lines sometimes bracketed his mouth, suggesting he'd experienced much hardship in his short life.

Fletcher rubbed his nose with his free hand.

Reading people had come naturally to him for as long as he could remember—nearly his entire life. The ability was as ordinary as breathing. Much like his interest in medicine had been, which had compelled him to become a physician, only to leave the field disenchanted and haunted over a decade ago.

He'd always admire and respect the individuals who made the profession their life's work. For him, the heartache of watching infants and children die despite his best efforts took a toll that seared his mind, scarred his soul, and left him drowning in defeat. It nearly drove him mad or to the bottle, hence his departure from the vocation before becoming an ape-drunk lunatic.

His expression downcast, Sean shifted his feet and covered a wide yawn.

"The truth is, sir, I'm knackered. My sister kept me up most of the night. Kimber's sick with a nasty cough."

"I'm sorry to hear that, Sean." Fletcher scratched the back of his neck. "Does she need a physician?"

Sean hesitated for half a second before shaking his head.

"Nae. I think it's just a summer cold. I left broth and a tonic. Paddy promised to keep an eye on her." Sean raised a thin shoulder beneath his much too-large black coat. "Forgive my rattling. I'd best crack on."

"Paddy is your brother?" Fletcher also made a point to learn something about his employees' families—those that had families. Many didn't, and it was truly sad knowing they had no one except fellow employees who often became their surrogate family.

"He is." Strong and wiry, Sean pulled the gold velvet

cushioned ebony chairs off the closest table with practiced efficiency. "Turned twelve last month. Kimber is almost eleven."

A wonder the two children hadn't been forced to find jobs as was the usual practice among the lower classes—probably due to Sean's diligence in providing for them.

It couldn't be easy for him.

Had Fletcher ever seen the lad without his coat or hat?

Even in July, the boy wore a plaid muffler around his neck.

In medical school, Fletcher had taken a few psychology courses. He suspected the boy's outer garments acted as protection from more than the elements.

"Did you know I used to practice medicine?" Fletcher finished his coffee and set his cup on one of the tables. "I could look at your sister if you wish."

Impossibly paler, Sean turned huge dark-blue eyes fringed with such lush lashes that women might become jealous.

"No, sir. That wouldn't be right. I know how busy you are. I'm sure she's on the mend already."

Fletcher understood Sean's distrust. Likely ashamed of his living quarters, the lad also probably didn't have a penny to spare to hire a physician. The boy had no doubt learned the hard way that favors often came with strings attached.

Perhaps Fletcher would give the lad more responsibility, requiring a pay raise. Though he hadn't been at *De la Chance* long, only since the end of April, he performed his duties with diligence and cheer.

Mayhap he could tend to the hats, cloaks, coats, and other items for the members? Currently, a maid did so, but profoundly shy, Sally preferred working in the kitchen.

Sean would require a uniform for his promotion, of course.

An advancement was something to consider.

Fletcher had permitted Bernicia Dough, the head cook, to send leftovers home with the boy since he supported himself and his two younger siblings. Sean never mentioned parents, and Fletcher could only assume there weren't any, whether due to death, abandonment, or perhaps incarceration.

Or perchance the children had fled an abusive home as Primrose McKessick—now his brother Leonidas's wife— had done. Sadly, that often proved the case in London's seedier neighborhoods, where poverty, unemployment, and alcohol often led to violence.

In any event, sending along food and other supplies wouldn't put Fletcher out of business. The world was cruel to orphans without resources.

"Good morning, Mr. Westbrook. Sean." Fred Brindlecombe, the concierge, poked his head around the corner before continuing to the front counter without waiting for a response.

Smiling, Fletcher patted the boy's thin shoulder and couldn't help but notice his fine bones. He was much frailer than he let on and undernourished too.

Fletcher made a mental note to tell Mrs. Dough to add extra bread, cheese, meat, and milk to the supplies she sent home.

"At the very least, I can have Mrs. Dough prepare her infamous tincture and a poultice." When Sean opened his mouth to protest, Fletcher shook his head. "I shan't take no for an answer, and if your sister does not improve, promise me you'll allow me to look in on her."

Though Fletcher no longer practiced medicine, he could diagnose perfectly well and obtain and pay for a physician if the child needed one.

"Yes, sir." Though Sean nodded, his guarded expression revealed he had no intention of accepting the offer. Nonetheless, Fletcher would persist for the child's sake and his staff's lest the illness prove contagious.

Fletcher turned to leave but pivoted back toward the boy.

"Sean? What time did you leave last night?"

Most people never took notice of the boy, moving about the club like a silent shadow. He might've seen or heard something untoward.

Tilting his face upward, Sean scratched his head. "About ten, I think. Maybe a little earlier. It was just after the fancy gent in the red coat arrived. The one with a ruby the size of my thumb in his neckcloth."

"Lord Huxley?" A self-important dandified coxcomb if ever there was one.

Artemus Fogwell, the Viscount Huxley, and his wife's presence had been a bit of a surprise. Huxley, the pompous windbag, had shown a decided interest in *De la Chance* several months ago—well over a year ago, in truth —but last night was the first time he'd graced the club with his presence until closing.

Surely, it was a coincidence that an ominous letter appeared afterward.

Wasn't it?

Fletcher made a mental note to apprise Torrian of that interesting detail.

"Notice anyone suspicious wandering around the private quarters?" Fletcher planted his hands on his hips.

"Sorry, sir." Sean shrugged again, causing his coat to brush the tops of his knees, one of which bore a neatly stitched patch. "But I left through the kitchen like I always do."

Of course Sean had. So he could collect the leftovers and the biscuits Mrs. Dough baked for the youth and his siblings.

"Very well." Fletcher narrowed his eyes, skimming his focus over the boy.

Perspiration dotted Sean's cheeks.

The lad didn't look at all well.

"Are you feeling quite the thing, Sean? I shan't dock your pay if you need to go home and rest."

"Not a bit of it, sir." Sean pasted a bright smile on his pallid face as he placed chairs around the tables. "You can count on me."

Morry Chandler, Fletcher's head of security and second in command, strolled into the main gaming salon, his expression inscrutable. Wiry and bearing a scar on his forehead that paralleled Chandler's right eyebrow, Fletcher trusted him implicitly.

"A word, Mr. Westbrook?" He slid the boy a brief glance. "Privately."

That didn't portend well.

Hopefully, Chandler might have information about the mysterious leaver of threatening notes.

Fletcher nodded as he crossed to Chandler.

"Do let me know if you see or hear anything out of the ordinary, won't you, Sean?"

"Aye, sir." His cheeks unnaturally flushed, the boy ducked his head.

The last thing Fletcher needed was for the lad to spread whatever ailed his sister and quite possibly himself amongst the other employees. Despite Sean's reluctance, wisdom decreed Fletcher ought to take the boy home and check on his sister.

Yes. That was what Fletcher would do—right after finding out what Chandler couldn't or wouldn't say in front of the boy.

TWO

De la Chance's main gaming salon

A FEW TENSE HEARTBEATS LATER

From beneath her eyelashes, Siobhan covertly watched Mr. Westbrook leave. Her breathing didn't resume a normal cadence until he'd disappeared, and the tension in her rigid shoulders eased.

She feared she'd given herself away this morning.

The way Mr. Westbrook probed her with his bottle-green eyes, she felt certain he could see all of her secrets—see behind her carefully constructed façade and realize she was a fully grown female at seven and twenty.

Thank goodness she'd inherited her mother's petiteness, and with her hair tightly braided and pinned under Father's cast-off flat hat, she passed for a boy.

Fletcher Westbrook held to a strict code of honor, and Siobhan felt certain he'd dismiss her if he discovered her secret. But the truth was, she'd tried finding employment as a woman for three months with no success other than disgusting offers from even more repugnant men. By that time, what little money Da had left behind was gone.

Desperation drove her to don Da's old coat and Paddy's trousers and to apply at *De la Chance*. She'd almost wept with relief when Mr. Westbrook had hired her. Now, at least, she could ensure her stepbrother and half-sister wouldn't starve, and they had a roof over their heads, though the drafty single room they called home scarcely qualified as such.

Still, their humble accommodations were far better than the streets. If Siobhan scrimped, the food Mrs. Dough provided fed them and Siobhan's wages covered the rent and other necessities, such as a candle to teach her siblings at night.

Months ago, she'd given up hope that Da and Maura would return. Not for a second did Siobhan believe they'd abandoned her and the younger children. No, something awful must've happened. The not knowing was almost as bad as imagining all the dark things that had kept her beloved Da and kind stepmother of twelve years from returning to their offspring.

Only five years older than Siobhan, Maura had become the older sister Siobhan had never had, and she'd never resented Maura. Rather, it had pleased her that Da had found love again, after Mam had succumbed to a fever when Siobhan was eight. She adored having a little brother, and when Kimber came along, their family had been complete.

After Siobhan's parents' disappearance, Maura's sister, Finola Florry, allowed them to remain at her lodging house. Yet the gesture hadn't been entirely benevolent. She'd moved them to a single room rather than the two bedchambers and sitting area the family had occupied since arriving from Ireland last year. Finola insisted Siobhan also pay weekly rent, proclaiming she wasn't a charity—that she had bills too.

Kimber and Paddy performed chores around the boarding house for their maternal aunt: chopping wood, dishes, cleaning, laundry, and taking out slop buckets.

Finola said their unpaid work compensated for the low rent she charged.

What a load of manure.

Finola Florry exploited her young niece and nephew because they feared she'd evict them if they refused to do her bidding. It was as unlikely as the milkman delivering fresh milk every morning that they could find other affordable accommodations.

After finishing arranging the chairs, Siobhan made her way to the kitchen.

In truth, she felt poorly and longed for a cup of tea, but that wasn't what had her nervous as a cat on hot coals.

She *had* seen something last night.

In fact, she'd invertedly become party to the offense— all because she'd been offered a pound in payment—a veritable fortune to a pauper like herself.

When the elegant lady withdrew the innocent-looking letter from her beautifully beaded reticule along with a pound note, Siobhan hadn't seen any harm in delivering it to Mr. Westbrook's office.

"I've admired him for so long, you see." The beautiful redhead blinked her big brown eyes, framed by charcoal-darkened lashes.

Siobhan conceded that with his wavy chestnut hair, bottle-green eyes, and tall, lithe build, her employer wasn't an eyesore.

"Naturally, Fletcher requires discretion, as do I." The beauty laughed, a tinkling, well-practiced chime. "My husband wouldn't approve. You would be doing me a tremendous favor, child."

Lady Huxley had bent over, purposely exposing more bosom than was seemly. Her cloying perfume had sent Siobhan into a sneezing fit.

Siobhan held a very different view of adultery than her

ladyship. To her, marriage was a sacred institution. However, amongst the *ton*, infidelity was as common and overlooked as beggars on the street.

Besides, who was she to judge her employer, who she had gleaned in the short time she'd been at *De la Chance*, had quite a reputation as a rake? Half the women attending the social club sent him coy smiles and blinked their eyelashes like the harlot Jezebel herself in blatant invitation.

"Naturally, I trust you won't read the contents." Lady Huxley curved her rouged mouth into a siren's smile. "Such intimacies are not meant to be shared. But I don't suppose you can read, so there's no need for concern."

Siobhan had procured a bland smile at the unintended insult.

She could read and write.

However, if the love note had only been to arrange an assignation, why had Mr. Westbrook posted extra security this morning? And why had Mrs. Dough tisked and tutted at the market earlier about strange happenings?

What have I done?

"I cannot lose this position," Siobhan whispered, unwrapping the scarf around her neck to allow blessedly cool air to caress her hot skin. Since last night, her throat had become scratchier, and swallowing pained her. "I cannot, *must not*, become ill, either."

She feared it might be too late for the latter, but she mustn't go home.

Lost work meant lost wages.

Despite what she'd told Mr. Westbrook earlier, Kimber might well need a physician.

How much treatment and medicines would a pound cover?

Siobhan could save money by allowing Mr. Westbrook to examine Kimber. However, she couldn't trust her siblings not to reveal the truth about her accidentally.

That must never happen.

It was one thing for a duke's handsome, wealthy adopted son to show kindness and munificence toward Siobhan but another entirely for him to forgive her for betraying him.

Stupid. Stupid. Stupid.

Halfway to the kitchen, she stopped and dropped her chin to her chest.

She must tell Mr. Westbrook about the note and her part in delivering the scrap of paper.

It was the right thing to do, no matter the consequences.

Her conscience demanded it.

She wasn't, however, revealing her gender. There remained the tiniest chance Mr. Westbrook wouldn't sack her because she'd done the right thing.

And if wishes were whisky, everyone would dance jigs, as Da used to say.

After wrapping the scratchy scarf around her neck again, Siobhan pressed a hand to her waffy stomach.

"God save me. Greed brought me to this point." Not so much greed but concern about Kimber. *Eejit.* "It's no more than I deserve."

Regardless, it wasn't what Kimber and Paddy deserved.

Heaving a sigh, Siobhan changed directions and forced her feet to move forward. With each step, her head became foggier and her stomach more nauseous.

Outside Mr. Westbrook's door, she closed her eyes to regain her equanimity while reaching into her pocket and extracting the pound note. She might never touch this much money again.

Muted voices echoed from within.

Summoning every morsel of courage she possessed, she knocked.

"Come." Mr. Westbrook's melodic baritone bid her enter.

She pushed the handle and stepped inside.

He sat behind his big desk, seemingly relaxed, though he exchanged a speaking glance with Mr. Chandler.

"Yes, Sean?"

It came out in a rush.

"Last night, Lady Huxley gave me a pound to deliver a

letter to you with arrangements for an assignation." Flames licked Siobhan's cheeks, although whether from embarrassment or fever, Siobhan did not know.

At this juncture, she didn't care.

Jesus, Mary, and Joseph.

It was all she could do to remain upright.

"I should have refused and come straight to you, Mr. Westbrook, or you, Mr. Chandler." She flicked the stern-faced head of security a short glance. His mien remained unchanged. "The truth is, sir, I honestly didn't know if ladies regularly made arrangements to—ah—meet with you, and I only meant to be helpful."

Was there a more delicate way to say arranged for a clandestine dalliance?

Mr. Chandler's mouth twitched before he schooled his features into neutrality again.

She marched forward and laid the money on Mr. Westbrook's desk.

Pray Kimber was strong enough to fight whatever ailed her.

"So you didn't read the letter?" Mr. Westbrook leaned forward, steepling his fingers and veeing his sable brows together. "Do you know how to read?"

"I do know how." Siobhan drew herself up, her pride stinging despite being at fault. "But I did not read the letter. It was sealed."

As if that explanation clarified everything.

Besides, Mr. Westbrook could easily tell she hadn't disturbed the wax.

"I made a stupid decision because my sister *is* sick and needs a doctor. But I am not dishonest."

Well, she *was* dishonest—even now, Siobhan pretended to be a boy, but only because she had no choice. She would not prostitute herself, and neither could she watch her siblings starve.

However, she did possess honor and integrity.

"That is why I am here." She lowered her gaze partly from humiliation and partly because he might guess how ill she was. "I'm truly sorry. I know I betrayed your trust."

Swallowing, she swayed and put a hand to her forehead, pushing her hat back.

Her head swam dizzily, and it felt like the very flames of hell licked her body.

"Sean?" Mr. Westbrook's voice came from far away.

Had he stood?

This wasn't good.

Not good at all.

She willed her feet to take her to the door, but they refused to obey.

Siobhan blinked, trying to focus her hazy gaze. "I feel so peculiar."

Her voice sounded strange—frail and wispy.

"I believe the lad's going to faint, Mr. Westbrook."

Is that what this sensation is?

Then, she was falling, her cap tumbling from her head as she sank into blissful nothingness.

Mr. Westbrook's voice raised in astonishment penetrated her stupor.

"My God, Chandler. *He's* a *she*."

THREE

A bedchamber at De la Chance

AN HOUR LATER

Neck bowed and arms folded, Fletcher stood beside Miss Kenney's bed—or whatever her real name was—and listened to Doctor Philbourne's diagnosis.

"I cannot be positive, of course, without observing her longer. However, my initial examination suggests Miss Kenney is afflicted with the ague and is definitely malnourished and exhausted." He removed his spectacles and, after tucking them into his coat pocket, pulled two brown bottles from his well-used leather case.

"This tincture will strengthen her blood. A teaspoon

once daily." He held up one bottle, then the other. "Give her a teaspoon of this every six hours. Administer hot compresses and poultices as needed when she is chilled, and cool sponge baths when her fever rises."

He passed the bottles to Fletcher.

That meant Fletcher would have to impose upon his female employees to take turns caring for her. They might refuse, and he wouldn't blame them.

He hadn't hired them to play nurse to a deceptive slip of a woman.

When Fletcher had risen this morning, serious concerns had niggled, but never would he have guessed the day's events would bring him to standing over an invalid's bed. By now, all his staff would know Miss Kenney had misled him. He, who took pride in being able to *read* people, couldn't tell this woman wasn't a teenage boy.

How old was she?

Certainly not as young as he'd first believed.

One hand on his hip, Dr. Philbourne regarded the slender form, almost as pale as the sheets she lay upon. Her midnight braids, eyelashes, and eyebrows stood out in stark contrast to her transparent skin. The thick royal blue counterpane tucked beneath her arms almost hid her chest's shallow but steady rise and fall.

"She'll require complete bed rest for at least a week and as much food as she'll eat, Mr. Westbrook." The doctor glanced upward, a graying eyebrow quirked in either awe or disbelief. "You truly didn't know she was a female?"

"No." Fletcher shook his head.

More fool him.

Not only had Miss Kenney kept her hair hidden, but she'd also bound her small breasts. That explained why she wore that godawful oversized coat.

Regardless, now that Fletcher knew her sex, he could scarcely fathom he hadn't detected it before. Her bone structure was too delicate to be male. Her voice, though sultry, was too high. Her innate graceful movements, which he'd taken as weakness in a lad, also betrayed her.

She was a superb actress; he'd give her that.

When was the last time he felt such an utter, sodding fool?

Though Fletcher presented a calm outward facade, inwardly he seethed with supremely controlled fury at her betrayal. Not only had Miss No Name deceived him from day one about her gender, but she had been duplicitous about last night.

The former was exasperating—the latter unforgivable.

The fact that her guilty conscience had prompted her to come clean meant nothing to him.

Fletcher would not keep a traitor beneath his roof.

Except, he must for at least a week, but after that...

Even as enraged as he was, he wasn't cold-hearted enough to turn an ill woman onto the street. Not only her but her young sister and brother. He wasn't an unfeeling monster.

Hadn't he already sent his men and motherly Mrs. Dough to retrieve Paddy and Kimber? Fletcher could hardly leave the children alone to fret about their sister's whereabouts or send a note along, which would likely cause as much upset.

Besides, who would care for them while Miss Kenney convalesced?

No, the best solution and a way of assuring Miss Kenney cooperated fully was to have her sister and brother right here at *De la Chance*, particularly since Kimber was also ill.

Mrs. Dough told him that twice when Kimber and Paddy had come to the kitchen to collect their evening meal at Miss Kenney's behest, Mrs. Dough had offered the hungry children a warm bun and glass of milk. On both occasions, Miss Kenney had worked late and fretted her siblings would go to bed with empty stomachs.

Given her thinness, it appeared she'd done that herself many times.

To ensure her siblings had food the next day while she worked?

No wonder she had succumbed to the illness.

When Fletcher summoned two female employees, asking them to bring a nightgown, he'd expected raised eyebrows and questions. The looks on Suzannah's and

Theresa's faces, after he'd revealed Sean was a female and they needed to assist her in donning the nightgown, might've been comical if he weren't so infuriated.

A knock rattled the door, and Fletcher opened it three inches.

Chandler offered a sympathetic upward sweep of his mouth.

He understood Fletcher's untenable position.

"Miss Kenney's brother and sister have been shown to a chamber to share. They are frightened and are asking about her. The little girl is quite ill. I left Mrs. Dough with them." Another partial smile kicked his mouth up on one side. "She's quite in her element, tending the ragamuffins. She's sent to the kitchen for hot chocolate and biscuits. I've ordered them baths."

"Very good." Fletcher nodded before glancing over his shoulder.

Miss Kenney remained perfectly still upon the bed as the doctor snapped his satchel closed.

"I want to wait here until she awakens," Fletcher told Chandler. "She is gravely ill, but I still intend to know her name and, if possible, what her intentions were."

Not that he intended to play nursemaid as she recuperated, for he did not.

He had three businesses to oversee, and now this nefarious situation with Huxley to deal with.

Fletcher would, however, post a guard outside Miss Kenney's door.

If she lied about her gender, what else had she lied about?

Her true reasons for wanting employment at *De la Chance*?

Was this the first time she'd acted on behalf of a Huxley?

No, he didn't trust Miss whatever her first name Kenney was any farther than he could throw her.

"Very good, sir." Chandler looked up and down the corridor. "I also spoke with your cousin about Huxley. He says he'll look into the matter and call upon you tomorrow."

Thank God for Torrian.

"Excellent." Fletcher pushed the door wide. "Dr. Philbourne, may I impose upon you to examine Miss Kenney's siblings? Her sister is also unwell."

"Certainly." The stout physician paced into the hallway.

"I'll show you the way, Doctor," Chandler offered with an easy smile.

As they strode away, Fletcher berated himself mentally for his gullibility.

"I can feel your rage from here." Miss Kenney's croaky thread of a voice scarcely carried across the room.

Fletcher spun around.

No more than thirty seconds ago, she appeared fast asleep.

Had she been feigning?

Nothing about her would surprise him.

"It's radiating off you in scorching waves." She regarded him warily but with admirable courage too.

Fletcher winced inwardly as her voice cracked and faded with each painfully articulated word. He'd not let her see he felt sorry for her. In truth, he was furious with himself for feeling anything but disdain and ire.

Compassion and empathy had no place here—had no business tempering his anger.

He kicked the door shut with a sharp bang, and she flinched.

Arms crossed and one leg raised with his heel planted on the wood, he leaned against the panel.

"I think I have reason to be angry, *Miss* Kenney. Or is it missus? Is Kenney even your real surname?"

FOUR

SEVERAL TENSION-FILLED SECONDS LATER

"Yes. I'm Siobhan Kenney. I'm not married." She licked her dry lips before giving a weary sigh and plucking at the coverlet, the only outward sign of her nerves. "I regret that I deceived you."

Swallowing, she gazed longingly at the water pitcher on a table near the window.

Hell's clanging bells.

Fletcher stomped across the room, poured her a glass, and then tromped to the bed, where he thrust the water toward her. "Here."

"Thank you," she managed hoarsely.

She drank the entire glass before sinking back onto the pillows, her translucent eyelids closed. Her pulse beat a frantic rhythm at the juncture of her delicate throat and collarbone.

From fear or illness?

Did it matter?

Fletcher removed the tumbler from her limp hand.

She slowly opened her eyes, despair and defeat darkening them to navy blue.

Despite his anger, pity tried to rear her head.

Fletcher ruthlessly tamped the unwanted emotion down.

He was the victim here, not Siobhan. Although, if he were perfectly fair, she might be a victim of her circumstances. Nevertheless, that didn't give her the right to lie.

"Did I hear correctly? My brother and sister are here?"

So she *had* been awake.

He gave a terse nod. "They are."

"Could you please stop looming over me?" She stared up at him, not nearly as intimidated or remorseful as she ought to have been. "I feel like you're an enraged panther about to spring, and I haven't the strength to defend myself."

Guilt poked his ribs, and the tenderheartedness incensed him all the more. Nevertheless, he stepped backward two paces.

She stared at some point across the room.

"Have you ever been hungry, Mr. Westbrook?"

He pulled his eyebrows together.

"Have you ever wondered where your next meal will come from?" she asked, cutting him a brief glance before training her attention across the chamber again. She idly toyed with the sheet's edge. "If you'll have a place to live the next day? Or if your siblings will starve because your parents did not come home one day, and you still don't know what happened to them?"

Fletcher mentally ticked off each question with a silent "*No.*"

She sounded as if she'd gargled glass, so rough and hoarse was her lilting accent. Fletcher didn't doubt that emotion and grief also clogged her throat.

Now, at least, he knew why she and her siblings were alone. He made a mental note to ask Torrian and perhaps also Lucius to look into her parents' disappearance.

"Have you tried to find a respectable position in an unfamiliar city, and the only job offered was to become a harlot?" she asked, though every word obviously pained her.

Fletcher suspected she bloody well knew the answers before she posed the questions.

He shook his head, still not trusting himself to speak or to give her the satisfaction of being right.

In Miss Kenney's mind, she justified her behavior and dishonesty.

Nevertheless, Fletcher valued loyalty above all else.

Her reasons might be valid to her, but it would be a cold day in Hades before he ever trusted her again.

"You might have told me the truth." He purposed to keep his tone gruff lest she believe she could manipulate him with her dire tale. "I would likely have found a position for you."

"You would have granted me an interview? A woman you don't know?" A winged raven eyebrow jetted high onto her forehead. "I have no notable skills. I've never held a position before. Pray tell me, how do you stay in business if all your employees are incompetent charity cases?"

She had him there.

Rather than give her the gratification of an affirmative answer, Fletcher grunted.

Siobhan shoved herself upward a fraction on the fluffy pillows, the effort costing her greatly. All the color drained from her face, and the hand she raised to shove a raven tendril that had escaped her long braids off her cheek trembled.

"You are angry, and justly so. I deserve a tonguin'." Her eyelids fluttered closed, and for a moment, Fletcher believed she slipped into slumber.

The next heartbeat, those fathomless blue orbs popped open again. "But when I tell you I had no choice but to impersonate a boy, I am not exaggerating."

God above, would she please stop speaking?

Fletcher expected her to spit up blood, so raw did her throat sound.

A glance at the window revealed the day would soon leave morning behind. Though he'd met with his staff earlier as was his daily practice, he must still have a word with his security before opening his establishments tonight.

"For months, I tried to find employment. May God strike me down dead if I'm lying." Raising anguished eyes to his, Miss Kenney released a harsh little laugh ending with a hiccupping sob. "You can judge me, but as you've never walked in my shoes or suffered what I've endured or feared for the wellbeing of others entrusted to your care, that makes you a judgmental hypocrite."

"*Judgmental?*" God help him. He was near his snapping point. "Someone could have *died.* Did that not cross your mind? I take the responsibility of protecting my staff seriously."

Each fury-tinged word cut through the air like the swipe of a saber. Though Fletcher appeared to be the target, that didn't mean others might not also get hurt.

"This is not a child's game, Miss Kenney. The peril is real."

Fletcher forced a calming breath into his lungs.

"*What* peril? I *thought* I was being helpful." Even in her weakened state, she glowered in defiance. "I knew you'd received previous death threats. But I understood that culprit had been apprehended, though you continued to implement an abundance of caution out of prudence."

How could Fletcher or Siobhan have known his nemesis had changed tactics?

Nevertheless, self-recrimination cudgeled him.

"I suggest you save your voice." Despite his determination not to let her pathetic story move him, distinct pricks of sympathy poked behind his ribs. Hunching a shoulder, Fletcher strode to the door. "The doctor said you needed to rest. You look about to swoon."

Had she been standing, he didn't question she'd have fallen flat on her face by now.

Regardless, he would bet she'd walk on coals before admitting how ill she was.

"I'll have someone bring you chicken soup," he said.

"What about my brother and sister?" Her voice had grown noticeably weaker, yet there was no denying the stubborn set of her jaw or the mutiny glinting in her ebony-lashed eyes. "When can I see them?"

"They are safe." Fletcher opened the door. "I shan't let you see them until I know exactly why you chose my establishment to defraud, Miss Siobhan Kenney."

"But they are innocents in all of this." Her exhaustion overtaking her, she sank further into the pillows. "Direct your ire at me all you wish, but I beg you, do not punish Paddy and Kimber for my actions. They yet grieve our parents."

His conscience whispered what an unconscionable cad he was into his ear.

This was why Fletcher had to leave medicine; he was too soft. Too empathetic. That was also why memories of his time as a physician still haunted his dreams.

Summoning his resolve, he raked her with an uncompromising glare.

"Be that as it may, I find it highly suspicious that you just *happened* to assist someone in delivering a threatening letter to me while pretending to be someone you are not."

"*Threatening?*" Siobhan puzzled her brow, the epitome of confused innocence. "It wasn't arrangements for a secret liaison?"

She was unswerving in her story.

Fletcher would credit her with her consistency.

"I do not dally with married women." His cryptic response earned him a skeptically raised arched eyebrow.

Widows, yes. However, husbands complicated matters, and he had no desire to feel a lead ball or sword pierce his flesh. Still, he didn't owe her an explanation.

"Then what did it say?" Siobhan appeared so confused and earnest that Fletcher waffled with telling her the truth.

However, she might be—probably was—playacting.

She'd already proven to be highly skilled in that area.

"It said, *It's not over.*" He watched her closely for a reaction.

She didn't disappoint.

Puckering her forehead further, she narrowed her eyes. "What's not over?"

"That, Miss Siobhan Kenney, remains to be seen."

Pale and surrounded by the large mattress, she appeared young and vulnerable.

"By the way. How old are you?" Most women flew into a dust-up when asked their age, but Fletcher was far past niceties.

Her glower suggested he could go straight to Hades. Finally, she sighed. "Seven and twenty."

"That old?" She glared daggers at him then, and despite the gravity of the situation, a chuckle throttled up his throat. "I meant it as a compliment. You look younger. Most women would be delighted."

"Well, as I'm sure you've gleaned, I am not like most women."

"Indeed." This petite sprite was unlike any woman he had ever met.

Then, before the sprouts of sympathy that had dared try to influence him had a chance to take root and grow, he slammed from the chamber.

What was he to do with her?

What a bloody conundrum.

FIVE

The same bedchamber

ONE WEEK LATER – AFTERNOON

Siobhan thought she might scream from boredom. She turned away from the window overlooking the bustling street and, folding her arms around her middle, paced across the gold and Persian blue Aubusson carpet once more.

The plush pile squishing beneath her toes felt divine.

This is only temporary, she reminded herself, lest she become accustomed to the luxury as she feared Paddy and Kimber had already begun to do.

She'd felt wholly recovered the past two days, yet that handsome, stubborn donkey's bottom who practically held her prisoner refused to let her leave her richly appointed chamber. In truth, Fletcher had ordered her to stay abed—doctor's orders, he said—but her muscles needed exercising.

Her mind as well.

Unaccustomed to idleness, Siobhan was ready to climb the walls of the lavish chamber furnished with a rosewood four-poster bed, armoire, dressing table, night-stands, sitting table, and two tufted gold brocade chairs.

Like the rest of *De la Chance,* royal blue, gold, and black accents decorated the bedchamber. The gold and blue brocade draperies perfectly complimented the blue velvet damask wallpaper and the trompe-l'oeil ceiling, complete with plump cherubs. Rather than overbearing, the color combination created an air of understated elegance, which was undoubtedly what Fletcher Westbrook wanted.

Last evening, footmen and maids had delivered a much-welcome bath and fresh nightgown to Siobhan's chamber. She'd washed her hair and let the mass hang loose to dry.

After so many months of hiding her hair—her one vanity—Siobhan couldn't bring herself to plait the waist-length tresses again. Hence, the locks hung loose, swaying with her aggravated steps.

At least the beast had conceded to allow Paddy and Kimber to visit each morning and evening, though why he'd changed his mind, Siobhan didn't have a clue. Kimber's ailment was nothing more serious than a summer cold from which she'd recovered. Paddy remained unafflicted but had acquired a serious case of hero worship.

Both children sang Fletcher Westbrook's praises until Siobhan was hard put not to snap at them.

"Mr. Westbrook bought me new boots."

"Look at my pretty shoes."

"Mr. Westbrook has Mrs. Dough make us different biscuits every day."

"Mr. Westbrook says we might read in his private salon."

"Mr. Westbrook is so kind."

"Mr. Westbrook is so generous.

"Did you know Mr. Westbrook has six brothers and a sister?"

"Mr. Westbrook's father is a duke."

Siobhan knew the latter two facts because she had struck up a friendship with Primrose McKessick before the former bookkeeper had married Leonidas Westbrook.

A pang twinged in her chest.

She missed her only friend, even if Primrose hadn't known Siobhan was a woman.

Somehow, she thought the newest Westbrook bride wouldn't condemn her but, instead, applaud her boldness and resourcefulness.

Did Fletcher think to use her siblings against her?

"Oooh." Growling in frustration, Siobhan fisted her hands. Moreover, the *roué* endearing himself to the children with gifts and attention could only lead to heartbreak for them later. Had he considered that at all?

On the one hand, while she'd been ill, Siobhan's siblings had fared well. On the other hand, she expected Fletcher to boot them all to the curb as soon as Doctor Philbourne declared her fit.

However, she would not pretend to be ill and frail to postpone the inevitable.

She would need to find another position.

Dismay bubbled behind her breastbone.

It would not be easy.

Not in a city whose streets teemed with beggars.

Neither could Siobhan take the children and return to Ireland.

Besides having no funds for the journey or relatives to rely upon once they arrived in their homeland, her gentle farmer father had confided that it wouldn't be safe. Something had happened to cause Da and Maura to pack their essential belongings, leave Ireland in the dead of night without looking back, and journey to London.

What that was, Siobhan did not know for certain.

She suspected it had something to do with the unsavory man who'd shown up on their doorstep several times.

Da always refused him entry and ordered him from the property.

Fletcher also made a point of dropping in daily—supposedly to check on her wellbeing.

She snorted.

As if he truly cared.

Each time, he questioned her as if she were a notorious villain. No matter what she said, she could see the doubt shadowing his green eyes. His distrust distressed Siobhan, and she despised herself for caring about what he thought of her.

Until a week ago, she had admired Fletcher Westbrook.

He treated his employees with respect, paid fair wages, and worked hard. She'd never heard him raise his voice, he didn't drink to excess, and he enforced strict ethical protocols at his club. His one glaring fault was his reputation as a rake—one she'd come to suspect might be exaggerated.

Truth be told, she had wrongly believed him an honorable man.

However, after a week of being treated like London's most nefarious criminal, her estimation of him had dropped to somewhere between maggot and manure.

No, maggots *in* manure.

The imagery caused the merest upward sweep of her mouth.

Yesterday, desperate for a change of scenery, Siobhan

had draped a blanket around her shoulders—her boy's clothing had *mysteriously* gone missing—and opened the door intending to see her brother and sister and perhaps borrow a book from Fletcher's library. Not that skulking around in nothing but a nightgown and blanket was the height of propriety, but on this side of *De la Chance*, midday, she mightn't even encounter another employee.

Fletcher had driven her to take dire actions.

However, Saul, the kindly guard assigned to ensure she remained inside her chamber, took his duties seriously. Compassion etched his face, but he'd shaken his head.

"Mr. Westbrook says you're not to leave your bedchamber, Miss Kenney."

It had been all Siobhan could do not to give into her pique and slam the door in his sympathetic face. She hadn't even tried to leave her chamber today.

Well, that wasn't entirely true.

She'd considered escaping out the window, but up three stories and without a balcony or anything to hang onto, she'd likely fall to her death.

Then what would happen to Kimber and Paddy?

Releasing an annoyed huff, she paced to the door and pressed her ear against the panel.

Rustling and low voices outside the chamber almost sent her hurtling back beneath the bedcovers, but she'd had enough. Tilting her chin upward in defiance, she backed away until she stood in the room's center and faced the door.

No matter what happened, she would remain calm and poised.

Easier said than done when one stood in one's nightclothes.

With a soft squeak, the door swung open, and Fletcher sauntered in carrying several boxes and packages wrapped in brown paper and tied with string. Two more of his henchmen followed him, each bearing a stack of similarly wrapped parcels, which they placed on the bed. They barely spared a glance in her direction before leaving on silent feet and closing the door behind them.

Humiliation and guilt scorched her cheeks.

What must everyone think of her?

She'd deceived them all, but she could not regret her action. Desperate times called for desperate measures and all that.

Fletcher took in her appearance, hair billowing about her shoulders and toes peeking from beneath her borrowed nightgown, and his expression didn't flicker a bit.

She liked that about him.

He never leered at his female employees.

"Excellent. You're out of bed." He angled his head toward the door. "Saul told me you tried to leave yesterday."

In a break from his customary attire, which usually consisted of a black suit and crisply starched white neckcloth and shirt, he wore a hunter-green jacket today. The shade did amazing things—dangerous, alluring things—to his already too-beautiful eyes.

To distract herself from her wayward musing and to prove he didn't intimidate her, which, of course, he did, Siobhan jutted her chin upward.

"I'm not your prisoner, Mr. Westbrook. I committed no crime. Had I done so, I doubt I'd have slept in this elegant chamber the past week."

"True." Fletcher nodded, his affability making her even more suspicious. Up until now, he'd treated her like a viper.

He also set his pile of packages on the tidily made bed.

"Why did you cease practicing medicine?" *Stop acting the maggot, numbskull*, she berated herself. She hadn't meant to ask the question out loud she'd ruminated on for several days.

His features tautened, and he thinned his lips. Finally, he gave a small shake of his head. "I wasn't cut out to watch people die, especially children and babies. With every death, I blamed myself even though I logically knew I'd done everything possible to save them."

"Oh. I'm sorry." And she was. "I shouldn't have asked. Forgive me."

"It's far past time I talked about it." He lifted a broad

shoulder. "For whatever reason, I feel comfortable doing so with you."

Should Siobhan be honored?

The man didn't even like her.

"I've made a decision." He rubbed his nose with his bent forefinger. "Or rather, I've decided on a plan of action."

"Really?" Siobhan raised an eyebrow, trying to appear poised despite standing barefoot in a nightgown. That Fletcher didn't seem to notice or care rankled, which only caused her more confusion. "And how, pray tell, does that pertain to me?"

She braced herself, prepared to hear the words she'd expected for days.

Sure look. Everything shall be fine, Siobhan Moya Neasa Kenney.

Somehow, she and the children would survive.

There was always a chance that Finola wouldn't evict them—at least not immediately *if* she hadn't already let their room. Only a numpty would gamble on that fragile hope. Finola Florry hadn't displayed a charitable nature thus far.

"You, Siobhan, and your siblings are going to help me catch the culprits who have been harassing me and vandalizing my establishments for over a year."

SIX

STILL IN HER BEDCHAMBER

"I beg your pardon?" Siobhan gaped, her mouth parted.

Fletcher might have announced they would have salmon for supper or drive to Hyde Park for an outing tomorrow for all the enthusiasm he showed.

"You. Are. Going. To. Help. Me," he said, articulating each word as if talking to someone without full possession of their faculties.

That assuredly had not been what she'd expected to hear.

It took another heartbeat or two for her to comprehend precisely what Fletcher had alluded to. He had best rethink his plans because no force in heaven or on earth would ever compel her to agree to his bacon-brained scheme.

Bristling, she shook her head. "Absolutely not. I'll not have my sister and brother endangered. You can get that out of your codpated skull right this minute."

"*Codpated*?" Wearing an irritating, half-condescending and half-amused grin, he leaned his narrow hips against the foot of the bed. "You don't even know what the plan is."

"I do not need to know," she snapped, tossing aside her earlier determination not to let him rile her. "Kimber and Paddy will not be a part of whatever hair-brained schemed you've cooked up."

He seemed utterly unaffected by Siobhan's heated declaration.

Feeling suddenly vulnerable in the light cotton nightgown, though he had never regarded her with anything other than polite contempt, she swept the blanket she'd used yesterday off the bed and wrapped it around her shoulders.

She tried a different approach.

"My sister and brother are all I have in the world, Fletcher. I am responsible for their safety."

"They will be perfectly safe."

He still wore that amused expression, and she was torn between curiosity as to why and slapping him until next summer to wipe his smug countenance off his face.

Where had the ogre of the past few days gone?

What had occurred to change his demeanor?

Narrowing her eyes, Siobhan breathed deeply, trying to decipher if he smelled of spirits. She leaned forward and sniffed. "Are you pished?"

Away with the fairies?

Crazy?

"No." Laughing, Fletcher shook his head, causing a chestnut lock to plop onto his forehead. "Not a bit of it. My, you are a suspicious little thing. Even more so than Clemmons."

Siobhan gasped in affront. "*I'm* suspicious? You've kept me imprisoned because you're convinced I conspired against you when I did no such thing."

Fletcher's secretary, Dawson Clemmons, wasn't suspicious. The man was superstitious to such an extent that it bordered on absurd. Last week, he'd exited the club and walked around to another entrance rather than walk beneath a ladder.

A knock rattled the door, and Siobhan took the opportunity to wrangle her emotions under control.

"Come in," Fletcher bid without the slightest hesitation.

Awful presumptuous of him since it was her chamber, but then again, he owned the building, and she was logical enough to acknowledge she had no power here.

Saul opened the door, allowing a fresh-faced, slightly out-of-breath maid to enter, bearing a loaded serving tray.

"Please set the tray on the table," Fletcher said, completely at ease, even though he stood in a lady's bedchamber with the dishabille occupant. Probably not for the first time, which explained the maid's indifference.

Why that knowledge vexed, Siobhan did not understand.

"We'll see to the rest, Sally." Fletcher flashed one of his stammer-causing smiles, and the girl blushed.

For pity's sake.

Siobhan nearly rolled her eyes.

He was as transparent as glass. For a man who insisted on scrupulous behavior in his clubs, the hypocrite had no compunction about using his charm to manipulate willy-nilly.

If he snapped his fingers, did every female jump to do his bidding?

Siobhan would not be impressed that he knew the maid's name. Something only a caring employer would make an effort to know.

"Yes, sir." Once she'd done as bid and given Siobhan a curiosity-filled glance from beneath her lashes, Sally bobbed a curtsy and departed.

"Come, Siobhan." Fletcher gestured to the table. "Have a seat, and while we dine, I'll explain what I intend."

The tiniest morsel of hope that he wouldn't dismiss her forthright motivated Siobhan to cross the carpet and sit. That and she was so hungry, her stomach gnawed her spin. "I'm so famished, my belly thinks my throat has been cut."

Fletcher threw back his head, exposing the strong column of his throat, and laughed heartily.

Transfixed, Siobhan stared as if bewitched.

Jesus, Mary, and Joseph, the man was a feast for feminine eyes when he laughed, which he did often, given the fine lines framing his eyes. In point of fact, Fletcher Westbrook was quite easy to gaze upon at any time, but he seemed oblivious to his good looks.

After composing himself but still chuckling now and again, Fletcher lifted the first silver dome, and her mouth watered.

Roasted chicken with peas, carrots, and potatoes.

Another contained creamed asparagus. A third held steaming rolls. And the last displayed thick slices of custard pie. A bottle of wine, glasses, plates, napkins, and eating utensils completed the sumptuous spread.

What appeared to be genuine kindness crinkled the corners of his arresting eyes as he skillfully uncorked the wine bottle. Siobhan had seen green eyes often in Ireland but not Fletcher's clear-bottle green shade. It took a person's breath away.

Surely, she wasn't the only one to react so strongly to his potent, verdant gaze.

"I thought you might be hungry, given you haven't eaten much all week." He poured a generous portion of crimson wine into each glass.

"Ravenous." Siobhan couldn't prevent her grin as she seized a roll and veered her attention to the bed.

Despite herself, her attention kept drifting to the neatly tied parcels littering her bed.

She'd heard tales of English Christmas and birthday celebrations where children received stacks of gifts. She'd only ever received one small object for either. Perhaps a hair ribbon, bar of perfumed soap, or hand-knitted scarf.

"What is in the packages?" Siobhan could have bitten her tongue in two for speaking her thoughts aloud. Mortification's flames licked her cheeks as she forced herself to focus on the food before her.

"Gowns. Underthings. Shoes. Hairpins. Reticules. A brush. Soap." Shrugging, Fletcher snapped his napkin open and placed it on his long legs. "Whatever else a lady might need for her toilet. I had the hostesses help with the shopping, so I'm not entirely certain what is there. I tasked Miss Rudgate with acquiring the essentials."

Elora Rudgate, the serving and social staff supervisor's extraordinary organizational skills, made up for her prudish comportment. Siobhan didn't question that the packages contained every last item a young woman would require.

She sat back, the roll dangling from her fingertips.

"Just what *is* this plan of yours, Fletcher Westbrook?"

She expected to sleuth around darkened nooks. She'd have no need for new clothing for that.

Fletcher cut a generous slice of chicken and deposited it on her plate before adding a liberal portion of vegetables.

"You and your siblings are going to help me catch the Huxleys red-handed." He glanced upward, catching her gaze with his. "If we succeed, I'll overlook your indiscretion and not only provide you with a position but allow you and your brother and sister to live at *De la Chance*."

Was he serious?

Why the change of attitude?

"I've already taken the liberty of having your things moved here. Your possessions are in the corridor. Paddy's and Kimber's are in their chamber." The humor faded from his face, and exasperation replaced his previous jollity. "Paddy told me that the landlady is an aunt?"

Siobhan nodded. "My stepmother's sister."

"*Hmm*." The sound rumbled in his strong throat like a provocative purr.

Just what did *hmm* mean?

"In any event," he said, "she insisted you owed back

rents and demanded I pay her before I could take your belongings."

"That's a colossal lie." The fib caused something inside Siobhan to snap, and she stomped her foot. "I didn't owe rent again until next week."

He rolled his shoulder as he applied himself to his food. "I suspected as much. I thought it important for the children to have their things."

Meager as they were.

As if sensing Siobhan's continued hesitation, Fletcher raised his focus from his plate. The intensity in his eyes took her breath away.

"What do you say, Siobhan?"

What *could* she say?

He'd provided her a way to redeem herself in his esti-mation—something that shouldn't be as important as it had become—as well as promised to furnish her with luxurious living accommodations beyond anything she could ever provide for her brother and sister. It was far more than she deserved, and she'd be an *eejit* to refuse this opportunity.

Which he likely counted on.

Her pulse quickened with exhilaration, yet wisdom demanded she tread warily. "All I have to do is help you catch the Huxleys in action? Nothing else?"

"*Uh-hum.*" Chewing, Fletcher nodded before taking a

sip of wine. "However, we must gather enough evidence to convict them in a court of law."

Did Siobhan dare add a stipulation to his magnanimous offer?

She angled her head.

"I don't want Paddy or Kimber involved." She rushed on before he could reply. "I'll do whatever you request of me, but I shan't allow them to be put at risk.".

Still holding the roll, which she had quite shredded in her agitation, and her stomach quivering with anticipation and hunger, she held her breath.

Leaning back, his eyes slightly narrowed, Fletcher tapped his fingertips on the table. At last, when Siobhan conceded he would refuse her demand, he sat forward and cut himself another piece of chicken. "Agreed."

Relief washed over her, and she barely checked a joyful whoop.

Mayhap, just mayhap, everything would be all right.

And Siobhan would do her part, whatever it might be, as long as it wasn't illegal or immoral.

Surely, whatever Fletcher required of her couldn't be that difficult or perilous. Lady Huxley didn't seem dangerous, just coquettish, and from what Siobhan had seen of her dandified fop of a husband, Lord Huxley didn't appear as if he could intimidate a mouse.

Siobhan pointed her fork at Fletcher. "And I'm highly suspicious about your complete change in attitude. How do I know this isn't some perverse way of getting even with me?"

Something akin to displeasure darkened his face's contours. "I am not punitive or vindictive. Let's just say someone very practically pointed out that had our circumstances been reversed, I might've acted precisely as you have."

"Who?"

"My brother, Darius." Fletcher took a long swallow of the excellent wine. "He arrived in Towne late last night. He recently left His Majesty's Navy and is at loose ends until he decides what his future holds."

Siobhan knew that detail.

Darius and Cassius had visited in May.

"Eat, Siobhan." Fletcher swept long fingers toward her plate. "You're far too thin."

A retort sprang to her lips, but instead of scolding him, she grinned and speared a carrot with her fork. She *was* too thin, and the realization she could eat her fill made her almost giddy. No more going without and saving food for the children.

"You'd better be careful, Fletcher. I'll be plump as a partridge in a trice."

He returned her smile, which also made her realize, to her consternation, that she liked him.

Really liked him.

Clearing her throat, Siobhan asked, "When does this plan get put into motion, Fletcher?"

"In a week. It will give us time to prepare you." He cut her a sidelong glance. "If you're feeling fully recovered."

She nodded. "I am quite well now."

Though her curiosity demanded she ask what her new position would be, Siobhan decided prudence required restraint. She'd already pushed her luck by refusing to allow the children to be involved.

She bit into a tender, herb-seasoned bite of chicken.

Scrumptious.

Yes, she could become accustomed to this life.

"What, precisely, is my role in this plan of yours?" she asked.

Fletcher skewed his mouth to the side. "You will keep Lord Huxley entertained, plying him with drink and compliments, flirting and making yourself agreeable, while I do the same with his wife."

SEVEN

Fletcher squelched the chuckle rising to his throat at Siobhan's flabbergasted expression.

"But...but I do not know how to flirt," she blurted before flicking a hand up and down before her. "And in case you haven't noticed, I'm not exactly the epitome of alluring femininity."

Her honesty and lack of effect charmed Fletcher despite his week-long irritation with her, and he laughed at her protestations, which earned him a fierce glower.

With that mass of midnight hair and eyes so blue they rivaled the ocean at twilight, whether she knew it or not, Siobhan Kenney was a beautiful woman wrapped in a svelte, petite package. This spirited Irish lass reminded him of Primrose McKessick. Both small, vivacious women, they possessed initiative, courage, and tenacity.

"Granted, you're not curvaceous." Probably because she hadn't had enough to eat in ages.

Siobhan pulled a face. "Thank you for that ungentlemanly observation. Every woman likes to know she's lacking in the areas men find most appealing."

"*Uh, uh*. Don't get your feathers ruffled. Let me finish." Fletcher held up a staying finger. "Trust me when I tell you that men *shall* find you alluring." He wiggled his eyebrows and lowered his voice to a seductive purr. "Even I find you quite tempting in an adorable weak kitten way."

"Go away outta that." Pink tinged her cheeks, and she snorted. "You're jesting, for sure."

Not entirely, and it was as much a revelation to Fletcher as her.

"I am not." He canted his head toward the bundles atop her bed. "Those boxes contain the finest gowns, slippers, fallals, and accouterments that money can buy. Your hair arranged in the current fashion, a touch of cosmetics, a dab of perfume, and adorned with jewelry, you'll have gentlemen lined up for the opportunity to make your acquaintance and dance."

"*Um*, I don't know how to dance." She made a comical face. "Unless Irish jigs count."

"*Hmm*, I hadn't considered that." He shook his head.

"It's of no consequence. I've never seen Huxley take to the floor. Bad knee or ankle, I believe." Mayhap gout. "He prefers the gaming tables."

"I do not play cards either." A wistful look whisked across her pretty, pixyish features. "Are you sure this is the best plan? I *could* help abduct him."

Fletcher burst into laughter again.

When was the last time he'd laughed this much?

"Why doesn't that suggestion coming from you surprise or appall me? No need to fret, Siobhan. I only need you to keep Huxley distracted. It's his wife I plan on getting the information from."

"Won't she be suspicious?" Siobhan took a sip of wine, and wonder momentarily brightened her face as she held the ruby-tinted glass up to the window light. "Oh my. That is quite delicious."

Her joy at something so simple caused a weird sensation in Fletcher's belly.

In all his years, he'd never met a woman as unpretentious as her, and he'd known many women. It wasn't that he'd believed her to be a male for the past several weeks either.

There was something about *her*—Siobhan Kenney—though he couldn't pinpoint what that undefined *something* was.

As the son of a wealthy deceased banker and adopted son of a duke, Fletcher had never known want or need. A large, close-knit, and loving family had always surrounded him. The closest he came to understanding Siobhan's need to provide for and protect her siblings was his concern for his employees' safety.

"We've considered that." He cut a bite of chicken. "Chandler and my cousin Torrian hatched a scheme to entrap the Huxleys."

In truth, wily and conniving, the Huxleys mightn't fool easily. Pessimism reared its gnarly little troll head, but Fletcher shoved it to the back of his mind.

Her expression unconvinced, Siobhan asked, "Which is?"

Fletcher arced his knife in the air.

"I'll tell Lady Huxley that my boy of all work mentioned he'd left me a note for a clandestine assignation but, regrettably, I never saw it. I'll tell her my secretary or one of the maids set it aside when they straightened my desk and fears they accidentally tossed it into the rubbish bin when gathering the news sheets. I'll claim that I don't want Samantha to think I ignored her message."

Siobhan gave a slow but doubt-ridden nod. "How will you convince her? You said yourself that you don't dally with married women."

"I'll persuade her that I'm interested in a flirtation and will make an exception for her." It shouldn't be hard to do. Samantha Fogwell, Viscountess Huxley, flirted with him outrageously whenever their paths crossed. Rumor had it Huxley was impotent, and his wife had strong carnal appetites. "Two years ago, before Samantha married Huxley, she propositioned me."

More than propositioned, in truth.

She'd practically begged Fletcher to have his way with her at a country house party—the last he'd ever attended. She wouldn't accept his refusal, and only approaching guests finally dissuaded her amorous attempts. He left the house party that night, convinced she'd have climbed into his bed in the wee morning hours had he not.

Less than a month later, her betrothal to Huxley appeared in the papers.

Siobhan's eyebrow shied upward, but she didn't feign shock as a society miss would have done. "That ought to make things substantially easier."

But then again, Fletcher wouldn't have had this conversation with a *haut ton* member in her bedchamber, let alone ask her to flirt with a married man. He'd have been slapped and probably called out for his audacity.

"I was involved with an actress at the time and declined Lady Huxley's invitation."

Fletcher might be a confirmed bachelor and rakehell, but he was faithful to women while he courted them. Besides, Samantha's desperation hinted at something ominous and unbalanced.

The cynical look Siobhan leveled Fletcher fairly

shouted she didn't believe him. "With the club overrun with your men, how will you arrange a private *tête-à-tête*?"

Should he tell her?

Yes. She would need to know.

"There are hidden, private passageways."

"Oh."

She left it at that, and Fletcher was grateful.

They ate in silence for several minutes before she set her fork down.

"I'm full to bursting." Siobhan dabbed her mouth. "That was delicious. I must compliment Mrs. Dough."

"You need to eat more." Fletcher eyed her still almost full plate and barely touched custard pie.

Giving him a starchy look, she shrugged.

"My stomach will only hold so much, Fletcher."

Did she even realize she'd fallen into addressing him by his given name?

That might cause raised eyebrows amongst the other employees, but then again, everyone who worked for him knew his strict rule of keeping relationships at his businesses purely professional. "In time, with sufficient food, you shall be able to."

She put a finger to her chin.

"As I see it, Fletcher, there is one major flaw with your plan. Everyone knows you don't permit your female staff to consort with guests other than respectable dancing and conversation. No one will believe you've suddenly changed your mind where I am concerned."

He winked as he lifted a forkful of custard pie to his mouth. "I don't recall saying you would attend as an employee."

That gave her pause, and suspicion tightened the corners of her mouth and narrowed her eyes. "Pray explain yourself."

"You shall be Darius's widowed guest because widows don't require chaperones and are granted leeway with decorum that a debutante would not." He circled his fork in the air. "No one will think twice about a woman he's escorting. It's also helpful that Darius went to university with Huxley's younger brother, so he acquainted with the viscount."

Because the Westbrooks were *so* important.

Siobhan opened her mouth to object, but Fletcher held up his hand. "Darius has already agreed to the plan."

Shaking her head, Siobhan placed her napkin on the table. "It won't work. I am not refined enough to pass as a *le beau monde* member, and you're forgetting my surname. Everyone at *De la Chance* knows it. Won't your other employees think it peculiar?"

Of course they would, but there was no help for it.

"Your surname presented a bit of a pickle until Darius suggested we change it to McKinney. As for the other staff, I'll apprise them of the situation, and they shall play along. They are tired of looming danger too."

To reassure her, Fletcher leaned forward and touched her hand on the table.

The gesture surprised her, and she widened her eyes. However, the jolt of sensation racing up his forearm to his shoulder nearly made him yelp.

"It's not the most elaborate plan, Siobhan, but I think it might work."

"You've worked it all out, haven't you?" She pulled the blanket snugger around her shoulders despite the July afternoon's heat. "I may not have a choice, but I still don't trust you."

Trust was a perverse thing, too easily given, and often proved a double-edged sword.

"Then we are well matched." Fletcher set his silverware down, the merest hint of exasperation in the abrupt gesture. "Because, Siobhan Kenney, I don't trust you either. However, we must put aside our differences and have faith in each other to pull this off."

She searched his face, all her doubts and misgivings parading across her features.

What would he do if she refused?

She mustn't.

"Agreed?" Fletcher extended his hand.

Her focus shifted from his hand to his face and back

to his hand before, after another heartbeat, she slid her delicate palm into his. He could break the fragile bones by squeezing too hard.

"Agreed."

EIGHT

De la Chance main gaming salon

ONE WEEK LATER

Siobhan could scarcely credit the transformation in her appearance this past week or the treatment by the other employees when she'd entered the salon on Lord Darius Westbrook's arm.

"You're doing splendidly," Lord Darius said as he guided her to Viscount Huxley's table. Tonight, the viscount wore the most remarkable shade of eye-blistering yellow. He seemed to disdain society's dictates and wore whatever color he pleased. With his aquiline nose, paunch, and padded chest and shoulders, he resembled an over-sized canary.

According to Fletcher, this made five nights in a row Huxley and his lady had attended *De la Chance*. He was certain their frequent presence portended something ominous.

Across the room, Siobhan met Fletcher's gaze.

The merest dip of his chin indicated it was time to put their plan in motion.

Lady Huxley, wearing a scandalously low turquoise gown accented by a diamond parure set and peacock feathers in her intricately coiffed hair, sent Fletcher a seductress's invitation with her eyes.

From beneath hooded eyelids, he returned her perusal and answered her bidding with a smoldering upward flare of his firm mouth.

Siobhan's stomach performed a queer flip at the interaction.

I am not jealous. Absurd. Preposterous.
Fletcher's doing what needs be done.
That is all.

Lady Huxley's eyes flared wide as a pleased pout teased her mouth, and she glided forth like the proverbial moth to a flame. She had no idea she wouldn't emerge uncharred.

Her ladyship took the bait like a fat, brown trout gobbling a wriggling worm.

And thus, the plan to ensnare the Huxleys was launched.

Siobhan prayed silently that the scheme would work because she didn't know if she could pretend to be a lady night after night. She'd memorized an entire back story—all of which was absolute codswallop—in case Huxley or another guest became inquisitive. None of the details could be verified or dismissed.

That tidbit had been Fletcher's doing, and she had to admit it was wise.

He advised fawning over Huxley while saying as little as possible.

She couldn't fawn any better than she could flirt.

"My dear, please enjoy yourself. I'm certain Lord Huxley won't mind if you sit beside him." Lord Darius released her elbow at Huxley's table, and as prearranged, a guest rose—one of his cousin Torrian's agents—and vacated a chair. "I beg your indulgence. I have an unexpected, urgent matter to attend to. I'll return when I can."

"Oh, la. You needn't fret on my account." Siobhan fluttered her hand-painted lace fan. "I'm sure these handsome gentlemen won't mind if I sit at their table, even if I do not play."

The four other players—all men—gave her a preoccupied glance before returning their attention to the cards they held close to their chests.

Gambler's obsession.

The cards had the men well in their talons.

Huxley veered his gaze upward, but his attention froze

when he focused on Siobhan. "Indeed, young Westbrook. I would be happy to entertain the lady. Mayhap she'll bring me luck. God knows my wife doesn't."

His sarcasm earned a round of droll, masculine chuckles.

"Heard you'd left His Majesty's service." Huxley shifted his focus to Lord Darius for a half second. Lord Huxley's comment seemed casual enough, but something about his tone raised Siobhan's nape hairs. "Plan on taking on an active role in your brother's clubs now?"

"Good Lord, no." Lord Darius shook his head, doing a splendid job of pretending horror. "My interests lie elsewhere. However, I'm not above enjoying myself for a spell."

Huxley grunted. "So who is this enchanting creature?"

"Forgive my manners." Contriteness puckering his face, Lord Darius put a hand to his chest. "Mrs. Siobhan McKinney, please allow me to introduce you to Artemus Fogwell, Viscount Huxley. Lord Huxley, Mrs. Siobhan McKinney. I'll allow you to introduce her to the others, my lord. She's newly arrived in London after two years of mourning her husband's passing. Her mother and my mother attended the same finishing school, and I've been tasked with introducing her to London's more respectable establishments."

Huxley made a noncommittal noise in his throat but nodded, his buggy eyes glinting with interest.

"Gentlemen." Lord Darius gave a short bow before departing.

Not one of the other men acknowledged his farewell, nor did Lord Huxley introduce Siobhan. Just as well because as fraught as her nerves had become, she would never have remembered their names. She could barely recall her assumed name.

Until now, she had never understood why gambling and gaming entranced so many otherwise sensible people, but these men gave her the merest glimpse into the addiction.

Da had played dice.

Too much sometimes, according to Maura's late-night scolds.

"Irish?" Huxley's peat-brown eyes lit up. "My grandmother on my mother's side was Irish. She had the most beautiful singing voice. A tear still forms when I hear a ballad she used to sing."

"I am, indeed, Irish, my lord." Siobhan produced a siren's smile and fluttered her eyelashes. Lord, she probably looked like she was amid an apoplexy. "I'm flattered you noticed."

"Come, my dear Mrs. McKinney. Make yourself comfortable." Huxley motioned for her to sit.

"Thank you, my lord." With a swirl of silk, she sank

onto the gold velvet cushioned chair. The same chairs she'd been responsible for putting in place each morning until a fortnight ago. Leaning the merest bit in his lordship's direction, she allowed him a whiff of her perfume. "You are *most* kind, my lord."

"Tell me, do you sing?" He darted her a sideways glance before examining his cards.

"Only on special occasions, my lord." She tipped her mouth upward. "But then any occasion to sing to a viscount would be *very* special."

Lord save her.

Only a dimwitted nincompoop would believe her gushing.

A pleased smile arched the viscount's mouth, but he said no more.

Several minutes passed as the players made bets, discarded cards, and collected new ones. Siobhan hadn't a bald notion of how the game progressed, but Huxley threw down his cards with a satisfied hoot.

"I win!" Huxley scooped his winnings toward the table's edge.

Disgruntled mutters echoed around the table.

Unexpectedly, after pocketing his haul, Lord Huxley scooted his chair backward and stood with his hand extended.

"My dear Mrs. McKinney, walk with me, would you? I'm fair parched."

As half a tumbler of brandy remained where he sat, Siobhan doubted he was thirsty.

Swerving a nervous glance around the room, she forced herself to remain composed. She wasn't supposed to have to accompany Huxley anywhere.

Not once had Lord Huxley spared a glance for his wayward wife, who still hadn't reappeared. Neither had Fletcher.

Did that mean things were proceeding well?

Siobhan refused to consider just what that might entail.

Chandler met her roving gaze and inclined his head as he and another security guard inconspicuously maneuvered their way through the crowd in her direction.

Stalling for time, she dropped her reticule, intending to notice its loss when halfway across the room and forcing his lordship to retrieve the dainty pouch. It only contained a handkerchief, a few coins, smelling salts, a small jar of rouge, and one very sharp hat pin for protection.

"Mrs. McKinney, you've dropped your reticule."

Huxley was more observant than Siobhan gave him credit for, and that disconcerted her.

She'd best not underestimate the man again.

"Why, yes, I have." She pressed a hand to her chest and blinked at him. "How remiss of me."

His lordship bent over and, wheezing like a winded

racehorse, retrieved the scrap of fringed cloth. Once he'd returned it to Siobhan's care, he extended his arm. "Shall we?"

Her heart beating a frantic staccato, she placed her fingertips atop his forearm.

He mustn't detect her reluctance.

"What part of Ireland do you hail from, Mrs. McKinney?" He took a circumventive route toward the room's perimeter—in the opposite direction of the refreshments.

"Outside Dublin, my lord." At least that was true.

"Ah, there you are." Wearing a broad smile, Lord Darius approached. "Forgive me for deserting you, Mrs. McKinney and for imposing on you, Lord Huxley."

"I quite enjoyed myself," Siobhan lied.

Huxley gave her the willies.

"It was no imposition at all." Huxley puffed out his jowly cheeks. "I enjoyed Mrs. McKinney's company immensely. Will you return tomorrow, dear lady?"

Siobhan exchanged a glance with Lord Darius.

"I should like to very much." She gave the viscount a coy smile. "But only if you shall also be here, my lord."

Jesus, Mary, and Joseph, she piled it on thick.

A familiar dark head across the room drew her eye.

Fletcher had returned.

Lady Huxley had not.

What did that mean?

Did Siobhan want to know?

He spoke to guests as he weaved his way toward them.

"Huxley." Fletcher nodded. "Your lady requests you take her home. She's developed a megrim."

"Of course she has," Huxley grumbled, not the least sympathetic to his wife's plight. "Never knew a woman to suffer so from headaches, and half an hour later, she fully recovers."

He bent over Siobhan's hand and placed his thick, moist lips on the back of her glove.

She barely suppressed a shudder of revulsion.

"Until tomorrow, Mrs. McKinney."

"I look forward to it, your lordship."

Once out of earshot, Fletcher murmured, "Meet me in my office in fifteen minutes. I have acquired some rather interesting information."

NINE

De la Chance – Fletcher's office

HALF AN HOUR LATER

Sitting on the gold brocade sofa, Fletcher rotated the whisky glass as he stared into the fire, one leg crossed over the other. The interlude with Samantha Huxley hadn't been unproductive, although he'd need more time with her before she confided in him.

The woman was petrified; that kind of terror only came from dire threats.

"Lady Huxley isn't ready to talk freely yet, but she's definitely hiding something. What's more, she seems utterly terrified of her husband." He glanced upward, a small frown veeing his eyebrows.

"You haven't touched your brandy, Siobhan." He raised one finger toward her glass. "It will steady your nerves."

She'd performed remarkably well tonight. Better than Fletcher could've hoped, but she'd confessed her nerves had taken a pummeling.

She dropped her focus to the finger's worth of amber liquid he'd poured into her tumbler. "I don't care for the strong taste."

"So we go through this charade again tomorrow?" Darius plucked the glass from her fingers and set it on the side table. He sat beside her and slung an ankle over his knee.

He seemed quite taken with Siobhan, not that he could blame his brother. Siobhan Kenney was a fascinating woman, nearer Darius's age than Fletcher's.

Not that, at ten years her senior, he was too old for her. But she was his employee in a manner of speaking and therefore utterly off limits.

That weird, undefinable feeling rooted around Fletcher's breast again.

He gave a contemplative nod in response to Darius's question before taking a sip of whisky. "I think we must. And every night until we've snared our prey. We mustn't let up. If you are up to the task, Siobhan."

"I suppose I must be." She mustered a brave smile.

"The sooner the Huxleys are apprehended, the sooner my siblings and I can go on with our lives."

As yet, Fletcher hadn't decided on a permanent position for Siobhan. She didn't qualify for typical jobs at *De la Chance* or his other establishments besides a cloakroom attendant. Knowing her as he did now, she would find the work tedious and unfulfilling, but she would not complain. Respectable positions were few and far between.

Still, he'd prefer it if she liked what she did, and that brought him back to what the devil was he to do with her after Huxley's arrest? Thus, for the time being, he kept pushing the question to the back of his mind. So far, no brilliant inspiration had struck him.

Her transformation from a skinny boy of all work to a regal lady was more than he could've hoped for. She mightn't have been raised among England's upper ten thousand, but despite her protests, she bore an element of refined breeding.

For certain, Almack's peeresses would find fault with her speech, manners, or some other inconsequential detail, but Fletcher had been hard-pressed not to gawk at her like a callow youth all evening.

Whatever seamstress had sewn tonight's sapphire gown deserved an award. The silk swayed and swirled with each step, giving Siobhan a graceful, confident air and accenting her gently rounded curves. The color brought out the blue hues in her midnight hair and caused some-thing magical to happen with her eyes.

In a word, Siobhan Kenney was stunning.

Several men had murmured their approval, and a couple dared to voice an interest in approaching her with disreputable offers. Fletcher had succinctly squelched their immoral contemplations with a glower meant to eviscerate, and he'd instructed Chandler to have security keep an extra watchful eye on the brazen curs.

Perhaps it was time to reevaluate the men's member-ships at *De la Chance*.

Huxley's acute and real interest in Siobhan was both a blessing and a curse.

Siobhan must tread carefully to retain his interest without leading him to believe she was willing to engage in a full-on dalliance. Fletcher, on the other hand, must convince Lady Huxley he *was* willing to engage in a romance without actually doing so.

It was a delicate game they played. One that could backfire and send their prey into hiding once more. Fletcher was tired of the intrigue and peril. He wanted the matter finished once and for all.

So far, Torrian hadn't been able to dig up a motive for Huxley's part in sabotaging and vandalizing Fletcher's businesses. The man was sly. Except for the note his wife had given Siobhan, he was always several people removed from the actual crimes.

What Fletcher hadn't anticipated and which needed careful consideration, was Lady Huxley's fear of her husband. She hadn't admitted Huxley was an abusive brute but confessed she was afraid to cross him and that he controlled her completely.

Except for her liaisons.

Lord Huxley didn't appear to give two farthings how his wife conducted herself as long as she remained discreet. Wouldn't her affairs incense a controlling brute? Nevertheless, men wishing to hide their abuse grew practiced at leaving marks where no one would see.

That truth put things in a different perspective.

Perhaps her ladyship carried out her husband's directives because he forced her to.

If Fletcher offered her a way out, an escape from the monster she'd married out of her lust for a title, would Lady Huxley be willing to reveal what she knew?

It was worth considering.

"I'm to bed." Darius rose and, after smothering a yawn, stretched his arms wide. "If you have no objection, Fletcher, I'd like to take Siobhan and the children to Gunter's for ices tomorrow. It will help build the illusion that I am showing her London's landmarks."

Fletcher's gut pitched at his brother's proposal.

Had Siobhon captivated Darius already?

Not a surprise. She was bewitching.

"Not a bad suggestion." Fletcher feigned indifference. "Except how do we explain the children's presence?"

Darius scratched his nose. "Could they not still be her brother and sister?"

Siobhan's face brightened. "Kimber and Paddy would adore an outing, but they don't know about my false surname. They might spill the beans."

Fletcher finished his whisky and then placed the tumbler on the side table. "I think I'd better tag along too and act as interference should anyone wish to engage in conversation. Unless you want to explain to Paddy and Kimber what our mission is?"

Siobhan shook her head with such vehemence that a curl tumbled loose and caressed her neck. "No. I still don't want them involved. They are unused to subterfuge. Trust me when I tell you that they couldn't keep the secret. Deception is not their strong suit. I could tell them we are using a different surname to protect us from whatever Da ran away from in Ireland, but that might raise more questions I don't have answers for. Besides, I dislike being dishonest."

That was another thing Fletcher had learned about Siobhan. Despite months of pretending to be a boy, her integrity was paramount to her. When she had a choice, she would always choose honesty.

"Let me know at breakfast. I'm fair fagged and need to find my mattress. I planned on leaving at half three."

Darius strode to the door and with a little wave, let himself out.

Fletcher risked angering her.

"I think you are underestimating your brother and sister, Siobhan."

She cocked her head. "Perchance. They are not little children anymore. Let me sleep on it, please. I shall give you an answer in the morning."

The mantel clock chimed half eleven.

Fletcher still needed to make a final walk through the club.

"Please excuse me. I'm quite tired myself." She rose and shook out her gown. "I'm unused to late nights and wish to look in on my brother and sister before I retire. I feel like I've neglected them these past days."

She had been rather overwhelmed with every kind of lesson and instruction Fletcher thought would make her ruse more believable.

"I'll walk with you." Fletcher ran a hand across his slightly rough chin. Not that he believed any danger lurked between his office and the sleeping chambers.

Still, it wouldn't hurt.

At least, that was the excuse he used to accompany her.

She shot him a surprised glance. "As you wish."

They ascended the two flights of stairs in companionable silence. Outside the chamber assigned to the children, she half turned, her mouth tilted upward into a tired smile. "Good night."

"Do you mind if I come in?" Fletcher grew more attached to Kimber and Paddy with each passing day. Their presence at *De la Chance* brought playfulness and a light-hearted atmosphere that he liked.

Siobhan's hesitation was so brief he might've imagined it.

She angled her head in affirmation before opening the door.

A lamp burned low on a table in the room's middle.

She crossed to her brother's and sister's beds, situated side by side with a night table between them. In truth, they were of an age they should each have their own chambers, but not until this business with the Huxleys was dealt with.

They'd had too many changes these past months, not the least of which was their parents' disappearance. Torrian had met with dead end after dead end so far in that regard, but undaunted, he continued to try to find out what happened to Maura and Tadgh Kenney.

Kimber slept on her side, a raggedy doll clutched in her thin arms and her unplaited hair almost as black as Siobhan's spread upon her pillow. Paddy slumbered on his back with an arm tossed over his auburn head, his bedclothes rumpled across his waist.

Siobhan pulled the covers over each child's shoulders before bending to kiss each of their foreheads.

Strong emotion tugged Fletcher's heartstrings.

Was there anything as beautiful or touching as a mother's love?

Or, in this case, a surrogate mother's love, for that is what Siobhan had become to her brother and sister.

For the first time in his recollection, Fletcher longed for children.

His children.

Siobhan glanced over her shoulder, and her gaze locked with his.

"Fletcher, why are you looking at me like that?"

Slowly, she straightened.

"Because, Siobhan, I am again reminded what an extraordinary woman you are."

He stepped nearer until only a few inches separated them. Seemingly of its own volition, his arm lifted, and he brushed a knuckle across one velvety cheekbone. "Every time I believe I have you figured out, you say or do something to astonish me and raise you higher in my estimation."

He hadn't meant to reveal his private ruminations, but just as he'd caressed her cheek, though it wasn't wise, his deuced tongue insisted on betraying him.

"Since your opinion of me is below sea level," she quipped, "I have a considerable distance to rise."

There, she did it again.

Turned the tables and eased the tension by way of a witticism.

He slid an arm around her trim waist, drawing her nearer.

Her mouth parted, her pupils dilated, but she didn't pull away.

"Not as far as you might think," he whispered, his voice thick and husky.

Blister and blast. I'm in it up to my neckcloth.

He should march from the chamber straightaway.

Eyes wide with wonder, she searched his face.

"Are you going to kiss me, Fletcher?" Her breathless whisper sent a thousand frissons over his body.

"I want to." Lord, how he craved the taste of those plump, cherry-tinted lips. "Would you object?"

"I should." Biting her lower lip, she spared a glance toward her sleeping siblings. "It would complicate things immensely."

Fletcher couldn't deny her insight.

But something told him it would be bloody well worth every complication. Every difficulty. Every impediment.

"True." Regardless, he took a step closer, her perfume and heat beckoning him like water lapping the shoreline. "But I'm willing to take that risk." More fool him. "Are you?"

She stared at him for several heartbeats, desire and hesitation vying for supremacy in her eyes. At last, she shook her head and skirted around him.

"No. I'm sorry." Her small breasts rose and fell in her agitation. "You have nothing to lose by acting upon your desires. On the other hand, I have everything, and I am not willing to compromise myself, this mission you've embroiled me in, or the wellbeing and future of my siblings."

With blue silk swishing around her ankles, she fled the chamber.

Fletcher lost track of how long he stood there, head bowed, and fingers curled against his thighs as he ruminated on her prudence-driven rejection and why it stung so fiercely. When he finally lifted his head, it was with renewed purpose and determination.

From this point forward, he could treat Siobhan like any other female employee, which meant she was off limits, or he could trust his instinct, which fairly shouted he should pursue her with all diligence.

And he must make his decision before he saw her again.

TEN

Carriage ride from Gunter's Tea Shop
Berkeley Square – Mayfair London

THE NEXT AFTERNOON

Siobhan tried not to notice the many curious stares or shared whispers directed toward the elegant landau as Baldwin expertly guided the burgundy coach down a cobbled street. With Kimber sitting on one side of her and Paddy on the other, Siobhan pointed her attention to somewhere beyond Fletcher's head.

The temperate July sun bathed the carriage occupants in pleasantly warm rays, from which her pink silk and ivory fringed parasol protected her complexion. As if suddenly wearing wide-ribbed bonnets and holding a sunshade would erase the smattering of freckles across her cheeks and nose.

This is a fairytale outing in a fairytale carriage, she reminded herself. *This is not my life or the children's. Do not get caught up in the excitement and forget your humble origins, Siobhan Moya Neasa Kenney.*

Kimber and Paddy thought it great fun to pretend to have a different surname to help Fletcher catch a criminal, but they were expressly forbidden to speak to strangers. Siobhan still held considerable doubts about whether it had been wise to be so straightforward with her siblings, but as Fletcher had pointed out, they weren't toddlers.

"The chocolate ice was delicious, but I want to try pineapple next time." Paddy grinned and bent forward to catch his sister's eye. "What kind do you wish to taste next, Kimber?"

"Lemon," Kimber answered without hesitation, a small smear of strawberry ice at the corner of her lip.

Siobhan quelched the worry that tried to rise at their innocent assumption that there would be a next time. "Let's be grateful for the treats we enjoyed and not want more already."

The children could not become accustomed to a life of privilege.

Even if Siobhan continued to work for Fletcher after the debacle with the Huxleys was resolved, her little family must live within their means, and visits to Gunter's for ices could not be indulged with any regularity.

And yet, this was the happiest Siobhan had seen her brother and sister since their parents' disappearance. Fletcher had told her he'd asked his cousin to look into the matter, but since Siobhan had no information to impart to him regarding where Da and Maura had gone or who they had seen, she had little hope he would be successful.

"What about you, Mr. Westbrook? Lord Darius?" Paddy's enthusiasm and broad grin proved catching.

"Oh, I always order bergamot." Lord Darius winked. "I've tried all the flavors—coriander, cinnamon, violet, parmesan, and the rest, and nothing compares."

"I disagree." Fletcher turned his penetrating, verdant gaze on Siobhan. "I'm rather fond of vanilla."

Which just so happened to be the flavor she and Fletcher had chosen.

A little thrill of delight tunneled through her blood.

A flush heating her cheeks, Siobhan glanced to the side. She immediately regretted it when two regal matrons in a passing carriage pointed at their landau, put their heads together, and spoke rapidly.

Fletcher didn't appear the least concerned about the attention they drew as the vehicle rumbled over the cobblestones. Likely as a duke's sons, he and Lord Darius had become accustomed to the rude gawking as if the Westbrooks should expect and accept people examining them in public like curious oddities on display at a museum, the circus, or a traveling show.

So accustomed to being invisible, Siobhan found it hard to keep her face impassive and feign indifference. She would never become accustomed to the scrutiny.

Thankfully, no one approached their carriage while they ate their ices beneath a maple tree's welcome shade. Fletcher's formidable frowns directed toward anyone who looked in their way might've accounted for that reprieve.

"Kimber darling, you have a bit of strawberry ice just here." Siobhan pointed to her mouth.

Kimber darted her tongue out and dutifully licked the spot clean. "Better?"

"Much." Siobhan patted her knee.

"Mr. Westbrook?" Kimber pumped her legs against the plum-colored seat.

"Yes, Kimber?"

Fletcher remained unfailingly patient with the children, and Siobhan fought to keep her resolve strong and her battlements raised against any foolish softening toward him.

Too late.

"How old were you when you ate your first ice?" the child asked.

He puzzled his forehead. "Four or five, I think. It was chocolate, and I remember getting it all over my face and shirt. My nurse was quite cross with me."

"Today was mine, Paddy's, and Siobhan's first time." The picture of innocence, she gifted him a brilliant smile. "Thank you for treating us."

Her pretty manners caused a small swell of pride to blossom behind Siobhan's ribs.

"You are most welcome." Fletcher met Siobhan's gaze across the carriage, and a scintillating current passed between them.

As much as this unexpected and new connection with Fletcher thrilled Siobhan, she was pragmatic, if nothing else. She'd heard the whispers circulating among the guests and female employees at *De la Chance*. He might be a wealthy, polite, and kind rakehell, but he was a rakehell nonetheless.

"It was my idea," Lord Darius teased. "Don't I get a thank you too?"

Her face scrunched in the way children do when they are in deep thought, Kimber considered his request.

"Yes. It was most thoughtful of you, Lord Darius, but I think you were as eager for an ice as Paddy and me."

Fletcher let out a hoot of laughter. "Smart child. She has you pegged, little brother. You have always been one for sweets."

Lord Darius released a good-natured chuckle and then winked.

Siobhan watched the exchange with a mixture of plea-sure and bewilderment.

When she had disguised herself as a boy, she'd never for a single instance regarded Fletcher in any regard other than her employer. However, since her ruse had been exposed and she'd been permitted to be female once more, she couldn't seem to stop seeing him as a handsome man. Far above her menial station, to be certain, but an exceptional chiseled and muscled example of masculinity nevertheless.

She'd have to be blind not to notice or so ancient she didn't care.

She was neither.

He was also the rogue quickly wiggling his way into her brother's and sister's hearts.

And mine?

HAT ANGLED to keep the sun from his eyes and also permit Fletcher to regard Siobhan from beneath hooded eyes undetected, Fletcher observed the play of emotions across her face. She tried to maintain a neutral, impassive mien, but her expressive eyes gave her away.

It was truly a wonder or perhaps plain stupidity that he hadn't realized she was a female sooner. She'd avoided eye contact and kept her chin down those first weeks. He understood why now.

In truth, the outing to Gunter's initially had him on edge, but as the day progressed without issues, he allowed himself to relax a jot and enjoy the excursion.

When was the last time he'd indulged in something so frivolous?

There'd been no more ominous messages or riffraff loitering around the outside of his clubs and theater, as reported by Chandler that morning after Fletcher found the disturbing note.

It's not over.

What exactly did that mean?

The harassment wasn't over?

The threats, fires, and attempts on Fletcher's life?

He had both Huxleys monitored so closely they couldn't pass wind or belch without Fletcher hearing about it. He'd have to give the viscount credit for patience. The man wasn't in a hurry to show his hand.

Fletcher didn't believe for an instant his lordship had decided to cut his losses.

No, Huxley was up to something and merely bid his time.

But why target Fletcher's establishments?

London boasted dozens of other gaming and social clubs.

This attack seemed personal, but why?

Could Fletcher convince Samantha to confide in him before Huxley acted?

And how long could Siobhan maintain her fawning ruse before the viscount presumed to pressure her for more? She'd likely punch him in the nose or kick him in the rear for overstepping.

Fletcher waved a pesky bee away, drawing Siobhan's attention.

She curved her mouth upward before presenting her pert profile and watching the passing scenery once more.

He'd been unable to resurrect his ire toward her.

In fact, his desire to protect her and her brother and sister had become paramount, though until this situation with Huxley was behind him, he refused to consider why that was. Fletcher never should have convinced Siobhan to participate in the scheme to catch Huxley, but it was too late now, and there was no turning back.

Should Huxley become suspicious, he might well retreat and delay months to strike again.

Fletcher was good and done with waiting and worrying, which was why he'd decided to go on the offensive. Tonight, he intended to pressure Samantha to see if he couldn't break through her battlements. He had another trick up his sleeve too. One that was extremely risky, but if it played out as he intended...

He'd have to wait and see if his instincts were spot on.

It was probably past time to apprise Father of the ongoings.

Fletcher did not doubt that Huxley would attempt to use his position to escape consequences once caught. Having Father on board and exerting his influence might become necessary—which meant writing a letter to Father explaining the situation and asking him to come to town because Fletcher could not leave London at present.

Too much was at stake.

The urgency thrumming through him to have the matter done once and for all had much to do with the three people sitting opposite—one spirited Irish lass in particular.

A confirmed bachelor who enjoyed the company of many women without regret, he'd begun to consider a much different future—one he'd never envisioned but which grew in appeal with each passing day.

A future with Siobhan—even if she didn't know it yet.

ELEVEN

De la Chance's ballroom

THREE EVENINGS LATER ~ QUARTER PAST TEN

Fletcher perused the teeming ballroom for a sign of either Huxley. Satisfaction ought to fill him at the number of people in attendance, but instead, frustration beat in unison with the pulse in his temple as he strode toward Siobhan seated along one wall.

As she didn't know how to dance—something he intended to rectify soon—she feigned a twisted ankle to explain her refusal to partner with the many men who approached her for the privilege. That way, she could still keep Huxley company should he put in an appearance.

Resplendent in an ivory and sky-blue gown, she fairly

took Fletcher's breath away. With every passing day, he marveled at the captivating little bundle of femininity. He'd begun to find excuses to seek her out, and even Darius had taken note, though his brother merely raised a cocky eyebrow as he slid his mouth into an irony-filled grin.

Siobhan, on the other hand, though polite, remained aloof and reserved, watching Fletcher with her unfathomable blue, blue eyes brimming with doubt and mistrust. Somehow, he must overcome her hesitancy. A task not easily accomplished after she'd witnessed his darker nature, but a mission he was determined to triumph at.

The Huxleys hadn't visited Fletcher's clubs since Siobhan met the viscount.

Fletcher's unease grew with each passing day.

He didn't doubt they were behind the machinations to run him out of business or that they'd hired Prescott to do their dirty work. Flexing his jaw as he strode across the sanded floor, he mulled over the possibilities that kept the Huxleys at bay.

Had Lady Huxley deduced he only pretended interest in her to glean information?

After hers and Fletcher's *tete-e-tete* the other night, had Huxley questioned her?

As taken as the viscount seemed with Siobhan, his continued absence might well portend a significant problem. In truth, a part of Fletcher felt nothing but relief that she wasn't subjected to the libertine's company. He never should have involved her in the scheme to catch Huxley, and now that he had, he seriously considered calling it off and figuring out a different way to catch the wily blackguard.

Fanning herself as she spoke to the matron seated beside her, Siobhan glanced upward at Fletcher's approach and gifted him such a radiant smile that he momentarily forgot why he wanted to speak with her.

Lord, she was a vision, but her loveliness didn't solely cause the warmth spreading through his ribs and tunneling into his heart. However, now wasn't the time to examine the growing sentiment. Later, when Huxley was dealt with, Fletcher would allow himself that luxury.

For now, he'd cherish Siobhan's geniality.

Seldom did she welcome him with such earnestness.

"Might I have a word with you, Mrs. McKinney?"

"Of course, Mr. Westbrook." She turned toward the elderly woman attired in a vibrant maroon and silver gown she'd been chatting with. An out of fashion mouche on the dame's papery cheek quivered with her movements like a fly in the throes of death.

"Mrs. Partridge, I have enjoyed our conversation. I do hope your little Miss Mousetail is feeling better soon."

"Thank you, my dear." Mrs. Patridge patted Siobhan's hand. "You've been kind to an old woman."

"Good evening, Mrs. Partridge." Fletcher swept into a bow before kissing her knobby knuckles. "As beautiful as ever."

"Flim flam, young rascal. Your compliments are wasted on me." She turned her watery gaze toward Siobhan. "Save them for this young lady. She's a breath of fresh air in an August afternoon fish market."

Fletcher laughed at the apt comparison. "She is indeed."

Taking care to remember her *sore* ankle ruse, Fletcher extended a hand to Siobhan to help her stand and once she was upright, looped her hand through the crook of his elbow so she could lean upon him.

It didn't bother him in the least to have her nearby. In truth, he quite relished the closeness.

As he guided her toward a private corner, he permitted himself the indulgence of enjoying her subtle perfume with a hint of peony, if he wasn't mistaken, and the way her raven hair shone under the illumination of dozens of beeswax candles in the crystal chandeliers overhead.

He leaned down. "Who, might I ask, is Mousetail?"

"Her cat. She's been ill, and Mrs. Partridge is quite frantic about her health. Lonely too, I think." Siobhan glanced upward through that sweep of sooty lashes. "What is it you need to speak with me about?"

Stopping near a potted fern and turning his back to

the assembly, Fletcher glanced around to ensure their privacy. This wasn't a conversation he wanted eavesdropped upon.

"The Huxleys arrived a few minutes ago, Siobhan."

"Oh." She darted a swift glance past his shoulders.

"Chandler informed me at once," Fletcher said. "I haven't seen them in the ballroom, and Huxley might choose to spend the night in the card room as is his preference, but I wanted to make you aware. Continue your ruse of a sprained ankle to dissuade Lord Huxley from trying to get you alone should he venture here. I intend to find Lady Huxley promptly, so if you don't see me for a time, do not become alarmed."

She gave a little nod, but he didn't miss the flicker of unease flashing across her features.

"I hope you get the information you need soon, Fletcher. I'm not comfortable with this charade or with Lord Huxley. He gives me the shivers."

As well he ought.

"I know. Neither am I." Fletcher shifted a few inches closer. "I've made sure you shan't be alone. At least one of my men will be near you at all times. Just don't leave the ballroom."

"I shan't." She tightened her grip on his arm as she peered up at him. Genuine concern deepened her eyes to navy blue, and it was all he could do not to draw her into his arms and assure her that all would be well.

"Be careful, won't you Fletcher? I'm not convinced that her ladyship isn't capable of great deception. I do not trust her."

Siobhan cared about him.

His heart swelled near to bursting at what she'd unintentionally revealed.

"We are of the same mind there." Fletcher rotated them toward the dancers. "Do you want to return to where you were sitting? It seems Mrs. Partridge has left."

The dame seldom stayed past eleven.

Siobhan shook her head. "No, that bench just there is fine."

She pointed to a tufted gold and royal blue bench between two more potted plants.

After seeing her settled, Fletcher braced his hands on his hips. "Would you like anything before I go? Lemonade? Ratafia?"

A kiss?

Her comfort, safety, and happiness had become paramount to him these past days. It wasn't wise, of course, but this feeling prompting Fletcher—almost against his will and logic—to pursue and care for Siobhan was unlike anything he—a practiced rake—had ever experienced.

Even he recognized the rarity and need to treasure whatever this thing was blossoming between them. It was almost as disturbing as the threat to his establishment but in an exhilarating, anticipatory way rather than dread and apprehension. Self-derision tried to skew his mouth upward, but fearing Siobhan would misinterpret, he kept his face neutral.

"No. I am fine. Oh." She looked beyond him, her expressive eyes telling him who was there before she spoke the words. "Lady Huxley approaches."

"Remember what I said, Siobhan."

"I shall."

Fletcher pivoted and crossed to meet her ladyship. He didn't want her near Siobhan, not that he believed she'd recognize the refined young woman as the ragamuffin to which she'd given a note.

He could scarcely see the resemblance any longer.

"My lady. It is wonderful to see you." He bent into a toady's bow. "I missed your company."

Always one to love attention, Viscountess Huxley preened at his fawning.

Fletcher swore she'd dampened her crimson gown, leaving little to the imagination. Rubies and diamonds glittered at her throat and ears, complimented by dual bracelets at her wrists. A velvet, fringed reticule also hung from her wrist.

"Dance with me?" He extended his elbow.

Lady Huxley wasn't of a mind to cooperate.

"Mr. Westbrook," she murmured in greeting as she continued past Fletcher, straight toward Siobhan.

Bloody, deuced perfect.

Fletcher had no choice but to fall in step beside her. He wasn't leaving Siobhan to the woman's viperish tongue or mean-spirited antics.

Forming a moue with her rouged mouth, Lady Huxley turned her pouting gaze on him.

"Introduce us, Fletcher darling, won't you?"

He'd rather eat boiled slugs. Centipedes. Scorpions.

Still, what choice had he?

He must have Lady Huxley's cooperation.

"Mrs. McKinney, may I introduce Samantha Fogwell, Viscountess Huxley? Your ladyship, Mrs. Siobhan McKinney."

What was her ladyship up to?

Had Huxley put her up to this?

For what purpose?

The viscountess made a pretense of looking around. "Your husband is not present, Mrs. McKinney?"

Siobhan appeared suitably sober. "I am widowed, your ladyship."

"Oh, that's right. Forgive me. My husband mentioned that the other night." Lady Huxley gave an artificial laugh. "How silly of me to have forgotten."

Why would Huxley make a point of informing his wife about Siobhan? Particularly if he'd formed a romantic interest in her?

To boast? Gloat?

From all accounts, he was a warped ponce.

Lady Huxley sidled closer, inspecting Siobhan with an intensity that made Fletcher's nape hairs stand on end.

"You seem familiar to me, Mrs. McKinney. I feel quite sure we've met before."

Hell's bells.

"We could not have done." Forming a small smile, Siobhan remained admirably composed. "I have only recently arrived from Ireland, and Lord Darius has been charged with showing me the sights as a favor to our mothers."

"*Hmm*, I could have sworn." After a final lingering look, Lady Huxley clasped Fletcher's arm. "Let's have that dance, shall we?"

Without a word, he swirled her onto the dancefloor.

"She's a pretty little thing but too thin and pale." Lady Huxley couldn't quite conceal her jealousy. "I know *you* prefer your women voluptuous and exotic."

He had. *Until Siobhan.*

"Mrs. McKinney?" Fletcher puzzled his forehead but refrained from glancing toward Siobhan. "She twisted her ankle earlier. Likely, that is the cause of her pallor. I was checking on her when you arrived."

"Your brother couldn't have done so?" There was the jealousy the viscountess unsuccessfully tried to hide.

"He ate something that didn't agree with him and excused himself to lie down for a while." In truth, Darius was perfectly well and, hopefully as planned, at this very moment, offered Huxley's driver a flask of whisky to loosen his tongue. "I imagine they will call it an early evening."

"She rather looks like a waif sitting there." Her ladyship tightened her mouth. "Huxley seemed quite taken with her, but I confess, I do not see the appeal."

That she could casually speak about her husband's fascination with another woman said much about the state of the viscountess and viscount's marriage.

"I feared you weren't returning and confess, felt great regret that it might be so." Rather than respond to her criticism, Fletcher side-stepped a couple, displaying more exuberance than dancing skill. "Are you well?"

Lady Huxley gave a wary glance around, then nodded.

"Fletcher, Huxley is suspicious. We must tread carefully."

That complicated things to no end.

"You know I want to help you, Samantha," Fletcher murmured for her ears alone. "I cannot unless you trust me."

"He beat me. I am covered in bruises, though he makes sure they are where no one can see them. That's why we haven't been in attendance." She raised misty eyes to him as they turned upon the floor. "He's not sane. He's sworn to destroy you."

And Fletcher still didn't know why.

He must get her away from her husband, but not until

he had concrete proof. Somehow, he must persuade her tonight to tell all.

Fletcher glanced over her head, then around the ballroom with the guests swathed in their evening finery. "After the dance ends, pretend to go to the ladies' retiring room. I'll meet you. There's a back way to my office from there. We can form a plan to secure your safety."

After hesitating, she dipped her chin in a shallow nod.

When the dance ended, she slipped away without a word.

After ensuring Huxley wasn't in the ballroom and hadn't observed his wife's departure, Fletcher exited through another doorway.

If Huxley had grown suspicious this quickly, there was no time to waste.

TWELVE

Still in the ballroom

A FEW MINUTES LATER...

Tension radiated throughout Siobhan, tensing her muscles, cramping her lungs, and keeping her on the edge of the bench she sat upon. She couldn't shake the feeling that something about Lady Huxley's presence tonight wasn't right. Her disturbing questioning, constant shifty glancing about, and artificial smile unnerved Siobhan no end.

She didn't trust the pampered beauty.

Without intending to, she observed Fletcher's and her ladyship's progress around the dance floor. He seemed attentive to the viscountess but frequently swept his astute gaze over the assembled guests.

Fletcher always knew exactly what went on in his club.

So far, Lord Huxley had not appeared in the ballroom, not that the welcome respite eased Siobhan's edginess.

According to Fletcher, the man had a bad leg, so he'd likely made straight for the card room, which seemed to be the viscount's preference. Nonetheless, Fletcher had insisted she pretend to have twisted her ankle in the unlikely event his lordship asked her to dance.

Fletcher still had no idea why Huxley targeted him and his businesses.

Over the past days, Siobhan's concern for Fletcher's safety had increased until it became a thrumming accompaniment to her pulse. Her growing concern made no logical sense.

He was her employer, and it was the worst sort of foolishness to entertain a notion of anything else between them. In her head, she knew that, but her silly heart seemed to have developed a mind of its own.

Yet, she wasn't so stupid as to act upon these newfound feelings.

She had a brother and sister to care for. Her life, her choices, weren't her own. Her actions and decisions must always take into consideration what was best for them.

Still, when she lay alone in her beautiful bedchamber, she couldn't stop thinking about Fletcher.

The way he tilted his mouth boyishly when he smiled. The breadth of his shoulders and how the muscles flexed when he moved. Or the way his chestnut hair shone in the sunlight. The rich baritone of his voice...

Yes, he captivated her, but she was not—could never be—a captive to her emotions.

Siobhan shifted, leaning slightly to the side to keep Fletcher and the viscountess within sight. Across the ballroom, two smartly dressed gentlemen watched the couple with more than casual interest.

Fletcher's men spoke in low tones on the ballroom's other side.

A shiver juddered her spine.

A menacing undercurrent infected the merriment and cheer within the ballroom.

Did anyone else sense the disturbance?

The string quartet played the waltz's last notes, and with a speaking glance to Fletcher, Lady Huxley drifted away.

From beneath her eyelashes, Siobhan observed the viscountess's progress as she left the ballroom, and then Siobhan shifted her focus to Fletcher, who had crossed to the other side. He swept the ballroom with his intense, verdant gaze, his attention resting on her for a brief moment, and then, with an almost indiscernible nod, he also departed.

Hopefully, his efforts with Lady Huxley tonight would prove successful, and this farce could end.

The gentlemen observing Fletcher and her ladyship separated, one strolling after Fletcher and the other in the direction Lady Huxley had gone. To the casual observer, nothing seemed the least peculiar about their behavior.

Siobhan searched the ballroom for Fletcher's men.

Chandler slipped from the ballroom.

Not good. Not good at all.

She straightened, uneasiness turning her stomach.

A pair of plump matrons had crowded onto the bench she sat upon. Heads together, they gossiped and tittered endlessly. Siobhan eyed the wall she'd been sitting along earlier, but guests occupied those chairs.

Lord Darius had yet to return as well.

Another shudder rippled down her spine, leaving her chilled, and a knot formed in her lower belly. Even as she considered disobeying Fletcher's directive to stay put, Lady Huxley reappeared at the entrance.

So she hadn't sneaked off to meet Fletcher, after all.

With a furtive glance, the viscountess angled her head toward the suspicious gentleman loitering near the doorway. After a disinterested glance around, he strolled nonchalantly after her.

Siobhan bit her lower lip as she flashed cold, then hot, then cold again.

"My dear? Are you quite well?" One of the matrons squinted at her. "You appear most pale. Perhaps you should lie down in the retiring room for a spell."

The other woman eyed the sliver of bench Siobhan sat upon with open envy. "We could save your seat."

Take it, you mean.

She was as subtle as a highland cow mincing down Bond Street wearing the crown jewels.

In that instant, Siobhan made her decision.

"Yes. Perhaps you are right." She stood, and after making certain Fletcher, Lord Darius, or one of the many guards on duty wouldn't come charging across the floor to scold her, she carefully picked her way toward the door Lady Huxley disappeared through with just enough of a limp to put off anyone asking her to dance but not so much that she drew others' concern.

Once outside the ballroom, she drew a deep breath and tried to determine what to do next.

Movement and a flash of scarlet farther along the corridor decided for her.

She would follow her ladyship and see what the woman was up to.

With a swift, stealthy glance around to ensure no one watched her, Siobhan lifted her skirts and hurried in the same direction sans her limp.

No one intent on meeting her paramour for an assignation—in this case, Fletcher—did so accompanied by another man—a scoundrel from Siobhan's amateur assessment who portended no good.

A swift peek over her shoulder revealed none of Fletcher's men followed her.

She skewed her mouth into a small grimace.

So much for not being left alone.

Her heart hammering so hard the organ threatened to escape the confines of her chest, she passed several closed doors, including the room reserved for ladies, before peeking around the corner.

Empty.

Forehead puzzled, she took several steps into the vacant passageway.

Where had the viscountess gone?

Had she slipped into the ladies' retiring room after all?

Siobhan glanced behind her.

Three giggling women exited the chamber reserved for women's personal needs.

Just as she turned around to retrace her steps, Lady Huxley's sultry voice rooted her in place. "Why are you following me?"

Dread drying her mouth, Siobhan slowly turned around, favoring her supposedly injured ankle.

Expression haughty but etched with satisfaction, Lady Huxley raised an overly plucked eyebrow as she brushed her gloved fingers over the marble-topped table to her left. "Well?"

Where was that man?

Even now, did he observe Siobhan from the shadows?

And where was Fletcher?

The secret passage to his office was mere inches from where the viscountess stood.

"I wasn't, following you, that is." Siobhan fluttered her hand, pretending stupidity. "I fear I have lost my way. I have no sense of direction."

The viscountess's disconcertingly sudden appearance troubled her.

One moment, she hadn't been there, and the next, she was.

Equally alarming was Fletcher's men's peculiar absence.

Tasting fear on her tongue, bitter and acrid, Siobhan fisted her hands against the urge to turn tail and run.

Why hadn't she listened to Fletcher?

Because she'd been unable to shake the feeling he was in danger.

"And your wanderings just happened to be along the same path I took?" Lady Huxley certainly was a suspicious sort. With good reason, but she didn't know that.

"I meant to use the ladies' retiring room to lie down and rest my ankle. It throbs something fierce, but I seemed to have become turned around." Siobhan mustered a wobbly smile. "Perhaps you could point me in the right direction?"

A nasty smile arching her rouged mouth, Lady Huxley shook her head.

"Did you truly think I would not recognize you?" She pointed her attention toward a wall sconce before flicking it back to Siobhan. "It was a corridor much like this where I passed you the letter to deliver to Fletcher."

Siobhan barely suppressed a gasp.

A sneer contorted her features. "You clean up well for a street urchin."

Jesus, Mary, and Joseph.

Lady Huxley *had* recognized her.

What game did the woman play?

"As I said before, you are mistaken." Siobhan lifted her chin. She would not give this addled woman the satisfaction of knowing how frightened she was. "Excuse me."

"Fire! Fire!" a man bellowed from the ballroom's direction. "There's a fire next door."

Paddy! *Kimber*!

A deafening cacophony of shrieks and cries followed the unknown man's announcement as chaos erupted immediately. Everyone knew the horror of the Great Fire of London in 1666.

Siobhan didn't hesitate a heartbeat before spinning around, prepared to dash back into the ballroom. To get Paddy and Kimber out of the building. To find Fletcher.

This was why the Huxleys were here. The fire was what those men had been about. The monsters had planned this bedlam.

Why?

As a distraction?

That must be it.

Where was Lord Darius?

The other guards?

Fletcher?

Lady Huxley laughed, a maniacal cackle that turned Siobhan's blood to ice in her veins as she lifted her skirts, prepared to tear down the passageway.

What if the fire spread to *De la Chance*?

Oh, God. Please.

It might already be too late for Fletcher, the club, her sister, and her brother.

A wail nearly tore from Siobhan's tight throat.

She only made it three steps before a large hand clamped onto her arm, jerking her to such an abrupt halt her teeth clattered together, and her neck snapped backward.

"Let me go." Siobhan yanked ineffectively at the steely grip bruising her arm as the viscountess's henchman dragged her toward the crazed woman. "We need to leave at once. Didn't you hear? There's a fire."

I must get Paddy and Kimber out.

Still wearing that insane smile, the viscountess pressed the secret door's hidden latch, and the door creaked open a couple of inches.

Terror momentarily stalled Siobhan's heart.

Lady Huxley knew about the secret passage.

But how?

"Oh, rest assured. I'll be leaving in good time." Releasing a dramatic sigh, Lady Huxley flung an arm across her ample bosom. "You, however, will tragically be lost in the fire. As will Fletcher and this miserable club."

Renewed dread slammed into Siobhan.

She might be small, but by all that was holy, she wouldn't concede without a fight.

She dug in her heels, not that it did much good. The ogre towing her along was at least a foot and a half taller and double her weight. Nevertheless, she renewed her struggles. "I shan't go with you."

"I beg to differ." A snide smile quirked the viscountess's mouth upward, and madness glittered in her eyes. Pulling a small, ornate pocket pistol from her reticule, she toed the door open further with her beaded crimson slipper.

Just inside the threshold, Fletcher lay unconscious on the floor, a wicked-looking cut lashing his cheek and another splitting his lip.

No. No.

Please don't let him be dead. Please.

Pale as milk, he lay perfectly still.

Siobhan couldn't detect the rise and fall of his chest, and anguish eviscerated her.

He cannot be dead. He cannot.

Inside the dimly lit passageway, a pistol tucked into his waistband, Chandler appeared as smug as a cat with a fresh bowl of cream as he stood beside the other henchman.

"Traitor," Siobhan hissed. "How could you?"

"For her and money, of course." Grinning, Chandler shrugged. "I can retire with Samantha in style now—someplace warm and away from this stinking, dreary city. No more groveling for the likes of Westbrook, Huxley, or the myriad of privileged sots who look down their noses or ignore me."

His tone became increasingly clipped and ominous with each syllable as he no longer attempted to hide his hatred and animosity.

"Yes, yes, darling. You shall have your revenge." Lady Huxley soothed him like one would an irascible child. "Didn't I promise you when you agreed to help me, dearest?"

Insanity flashed in Chandler's eyes and contorted his features.

Heaven help me.

He was as demented as the viscountess—perhaps more so, *the devil's spawn.*

"You'll come along, or I'll shoot Fletcher now." Her ladyship pointed the gun at his head and, with blood-chilling calm, said, "It makes no difference to me if he dies now or in a few minutes. However, I think it makes a great difference to you, Siobhan."

He isn't dead.

Simultaneous relief and renewed terror hitched Siobhan's breath.

"No! Don't." Tears streamed from her eyes. How badly hurt was Fletcher? "I'll come with you."

"I thought you'd see it my way." Lady Huxley stepped over Fletcher's prone form as if he was an old house slipper or newssheet.

She was utterly mad.

Once Siobhan entered the secret passageway, her ladyship pressed another hidden latch, closing the door.

Apparently, Chandler had revealed everything to her, the rotten traitor.

Then why hadn't *he* delivered the note Lady Huxley had given to Siobhan?

So much of this debacle didn't make sense.

The brute holding Siobhan released her, and she dropped to her knees. Cradling Fletcher's head in her lap, she tried to assess the extent of his injuries. Blood spattered his neckcloth and coat. His chest rose and fell evenly, though his pallor resembled death and his breathing was shallow.

"Fletcher? Can you hear me?" she whispered near his ear. "Please don't die." She clutched his coat. "You cannot die. I haven't told you how I feel about you."

At this moment, Siobhan didn't care who knew her judiciously guarded secret—she loved Fletcher.

She brushed his hair off his forehead, wincing when the movement revealed another nasty gash. He hadn't gone down without a fight.

"Bring them along," Lady Huxley ordered as she slid her gloved hand into Chandler's bent elbow, still brandishing the pistol in her other hand.

Her beastly henchmen grabbed Fletcher beneath his arms and hauled him down the narrow passageway, his head lolling to one side and his heels dragging.

Siobhan jumped to her feet and followed.

A plan.

She must come up with a plan.

But what?

She was absolute rot at this sort of thing.

God, please protect Paddy and Kimber, and please help Fletcher and me. And please, please don't let the fire spread to De la Chance.

As Siobhan trudged along, she kept her focus riveted on Fletcher, silently willing him to wake up.

He cracked an eyelid open and, winking, formed his lips into a silent *"Shh"* before feigning unconsciousness again.

Siobhan gasped, causing the smaller blackguard to turn and glare at her.

"Spi-der," she stuttered and gave an exaggerated shudder. "I saw a spider."

He rolled his eyes in disgust.

The tiniest morsel of hope sang along her blood.

If God heard her prayers, *if* fate smiled upon them, *if* Fletcher had a plan, she and Fletcher might get out of this alive after all.

THIRTEEN

Fletcher's office

FIVE MINUTES LATER

Time crept by interminably slow as Viscountess Huxley, yet wielding the ivory-handled pistol, paced back and forth in Fletcher's office. Agitation fairly radiated off her as she muttered under her breath.

Though only five minutes had passed, each second lengthened into what felt like an hour. Smoke's choking stench and the frantic sounds outside filtered through the drawn draperies.

A myriad of questions pummeled Siobhan.

Where were Paddy and Kimber?

Had someone made sure they made it outside?

How big was the fire?

Had it been extinguished?

Was *De la Chance* at risk?

Were others still in the club and in peril?

Were she and Fletcher going to die at the hands of these lunatics?

Do not think about it.

She grazed her fingertips across Fletcher's forehead and down his cheek. Only to reinforce the ruse he played at, of course. Not because Siobhan couldn't help reassure herself that he was alive and, though bruised and cut, would be all right.

If they managed to escape the demented curs holding them prisoner.

That was a very big if.

The fact that none of Fletcher's security team or his brother had appeared didn't portend well.

Siobhan forced her thoughts elsewhere, for if she dwelled on the danger, she'd become paralyzed with fear, and Fletcher needed her to have her wits about her to assist him in whatever he had planned.

He'd best get to it, however.

If the blaze spread to *De la Chance*...

Setting a fire.

What a stupid and reckless scheme. However, it wasn't the first time her ladyship had employed the method.

It spoke to the absolute insanity of the Huxleys. Their accomplices too.

Through half-lowered lashes, Siobhan observed the viscountess and Chandler. Both appeared peculiarly at ease given the perilous circumstances. On the other hand, the brutes Lady Huxley employed glanced around like a nervous mother dog with newborn pups.

Fletcher lay insensate upon the sofa where Lady Huxley's thugs had unceremoniously dumped him. Pulse racing in anticipation of what he had planned, Siobhan had sat on the sofa and slipped his head onto her lap, only too happy to aide in his deception.

Why he pretended unconsciousness, she couldn't guess. And how the two of them could ward off the four menaces in his office also eluded her. Nevertheless, she trusted Fletcher implicitly.

The realization gave her an internal start.

She caressed his beloved face with her gaze.

She did trust him.

Wholly and without reservation.

When had her wariness and distrust changed?

Probably when she'd acknowledged to herself that she cared for him—no, not just cared for him.

Siobhan loved Fletcher.

She wasn't supposed to. She knew better. She'd tried not to. She really had.

Nonetheless, the emotion had proved too potent and intoxicating to resist.

She loved him so completely, unreservedly, irrefutably, and irreversibly that her heart could scarcely contain the emotion, and her mind could hardly comprehend the truth. Surely, her love must be apparent to everyone, for how could she hide something so powerful?

"Where is my useless, mincing fop of a husband?" Her ladyship sent a seething glower toward the door. It was a wonder the panel didn't burst into flames. "I swear. The man's incapable of even the simplest of feats. I must explain every detail to him, thrice over."

"Never fear, my love. You shall be rid of him soon enough," Chandler soothed before kissing her forehead.

Siobhan hadn't a doubt now that Lady Huxley had been the mastermind behind the crimes perpetuated against Fletcher and his clubs with her husband's and Chandler's assistance.

Did Huxley know his wife and Chandler were having an affair?

Had Fletcher ever suspected his head of security's disloyalty?

"Why are you doing this?" Siobhan asked.

What could motivate a person to be this evil?

The viscountess stalked across the carpet until she stood directly before Siobhan and Fletcher. "Revenge, of course."

"Revenge?" Siobhan puzzled her forehead. "For what?"

With a convincing groan, Fletcher stirred and fluttered his eyelashes before slowly opening his beautiful green eyes. His gaze meshed with hers as he silently begged her to trust him.

And she did. Without hesitation.

Groaning again and holding a hand to his head, he slowly angled upward until he slumped upright on the sofa.

Siobhan prayed he only acted and wasn't in as much pain as he appeared.

"I'm sure Fletcher can answer that question," the viscountess purred as she leaned over him. "Why don't you enlighten the skinny waif? She's obviously in love with you."

She practically spat the last words.

A flush heated Siobhan's cheeks, but she refused to refute the accusation. If she were about to die, she would do so with Fletcher knowing the truth.

He grasped Siobhan's hand in his much larger palm. He gave her fingers a reassuring squeeze, and she gripped his in return. Somehow, and as irrational as it seemed, his big, warm hand encompassing hers made her feel as protected and invincible as a wall of armored soldiers with shields raised.

A hoarse shout somewhere in the club drew Siobhan's

attention. The clamor outside made it impossible to tell where the cry came from.

A sinister smile twisted the viscountess's mouth upward.

"That makes my vengeance that much sweeter." She tapped her chin, switching her attention between Fletcher and Siobhan. She aimed the gun at Siobhan's chest. "I shall quite relish your anguish, Fletcher, as you watch her bleed to death, knowing you are helpless to save her and that you brought this end not only on yourself but on her —an innocent victim."

"All because I rejected your proposition two years ago?" Raspiness threaded Fletcher's voice as he affected weakness. "Is this what the vandalism, fires, and sabotaging have been about? Vengeance because I didn't jump into your bed when you crooked your finger?"

Arms folded and one hip resting on the desk, Chandler remained oddly impervious to the conversation. He'd undoubtedly heard the tale before from Fletcher's and the viscountess's perspectives.

One of Lady Huxley's collaborators occasionally lifted the drapery's edge while the other stood near the door. The entrance to the secret passage gaped open a few inches, though whether from an oversight or because her ladyship was confident no one would intervene, Siobhan couldn't discern.

And it appeared no one would come to hers and Fletcher's rescue.

Not knowing if Paddy and Kimber were safe cleaved Siobhan's heart in two. She didn't mind dying. Everyone did, eventually. She did, however, object to being murdered before she'd ever had a chance to tell Fletcher she loved him and before ensuring her brother's and sister's futures were secure.

"I was pregnant." The viscountess loomed above Fletcher, her eyes narrowed and mouth thinned. "I wanted to marry *you*, not that doddering, simple-minded fool! Huxley, the impotent sod, wished to claim the child as his."

The unscrupulous tart had thought to entrap Fletcher into marriage and didn't have a qualm about admitting her subterfuge. What made a person that wicked?

Siobhan risked a glance toward Chandler.

Her ladyship's confession couldn't be easy for him to hear.

His expression remained stony and inscrutable.

Anguish crumpled Lady Huxley's features. "I lost the babe, and the physicians say I shall never bear a child. You robbed me of the chance to be a mother, Fletcher."

Had grief caused her tumble into lunacy?

"I'm truly sorry, Samantha." Fletcher kept his tone kind and comforting. "The loss of a child is tragic, no matter the circumstances. But surely you must know, deep in your heart, that had we married, there is no guarantee the child would've survived."

"That's not true," she railed, completely unhinged. "It *is* your fault, and I determined you would pay. You would grieve as I have. I'd strip you of everything important to you."

"But why would Lord Huxley agree to this madness?" The question left Siobhan's lips before she could stifle it.

"Because the fool loves me and would do anything I ask of him." Lady Huxley cackled. "Love does that to a person. Makes them do things they never believed themselves capable of."

Was that why Chandler helped the viscountess, or was his motive purely greed?

Did love cause one to toss aside morals, decency, and honor?

Siobhan could not conceive it.

She loved Fletcher so much that it consumed her, but she wouldn't have committed crimes to appease him. True, sacrificial love made a person better, not worse.

Another chorus of dramatic shouts drew everyone's attention, and they glanced toward the closed draperies.

The next instant, chaos erupted.

Men burst through the windows, charged through the secret passageway, and kicked down the office door. In moments, Lady Huxley's outnumbered thugs were overtaken and subdued.

Without a second thought, Siobhan levered a forceful kick and dislodged the gun from Lady Huxley's hand.

"No!" the viscountess shrieked as she frantically turned this way and that, searching for her pistol. "Chandler. Kill her! Kill them both."

Fletcher yanked Siobhan to her feet and placed himself between her and the frothing viscountess.

Gun in hand, Chandler charged across the office, straight toward Fletcher, but at the last second, veered toward her ladyship and pointed the gun at her instead. "I don't take orders from you."

Jaw unhinged, Lady Huxley gaped before erupting into an ear-scorching string of foul oaths that would've made a seasoned sailor blush.

"Well done, you." Fletcher clapped Chandler on the shoulder as another man seized the viscountess's arm. "You almost convinced me you were abetting her. I think a substantial raise is in order, my friend."

What?

It had all been an act?

Siobhan looked between them, trying to comprehend what had just happened.

Chandler wasn't a traitor?

Pain sluiced Siobhan's heart as the unmitigated truth hit her.

A scream of denial tried to throttle up her throat, but she swallowed it.

Fletcher hadn't trusted her enough to tell her this part of his scheme.

What if this madcap plan had gone wrong?

They might've been shot at any moment.

Her hurt swiftly became scorching anger.

It was one thing to jeopardize his life and hers, but Paddy's and Kimber's?

Such fury heated her blood that she fisted her hands to keep from slugging him.

How dare he?

Fletcher didn't trust her as much as she did him, and that knowledge stung—no, it gutted her.

It was good that Siobhan hadn't declared herself to Fletcher and had no idea how he felt about her. It didn't matter now. She might love him, but the last few minutes made it abundantly clear love was insufficient. Love and trust were opposite sides of the same coin. A healthy, thriving relationship required both.

"I confess I grew a bit apprehensive for a spell, sir." Chandler swiped his forearm across his moist forehead. "And don't ever ask me to hit you again. I shall refuse. I nearly gave myself away more than once."

Was the private conversation Chandler insisted on having with Fletcher all those days ago related to what had just occurred?

How long had Chandler and Fletcher been in cahoots?

"Siobhan, may I introduce my cousin, Torrian Westbrook?" Fletcher indicated the man holding Lady Huxley's arm as the viscountess squirmed and swore. "He's a private detective. Torrian, this is Siobhan Kenney, the bravest woman I know."

Brave but not trustworthy.

"Miss Kenney." Torrian dipped his strong chin. "I've had news of your parents."

Siobhan froze, afraid to hear more.

Fletcher drew his eyebrows together. "Now isn't the time, Torrian."

"Normally, I'd agree with you, Cousin. But I've learned they will be deported to Australia on a convict ship in three days. They were accused of stealing a toff's purse and have been rotting in Newgate Prison all this time. Interestingly, their accuser is also Irish."

"They would never have stolen anything." Siobhan knew her father and stepmother. They were not thieves. "Da fled Ireland and wouldn't tell me why. I bet this man who has falsely accused him is the reason."

And she'd bet he was the same unwelcome brute who'd called at their house those times in Ireland. She darted glance toward the door. "I must go to them. Take them food. Clothing. Medicine."

Fletcher touched her forearm. "Do not fret. I shall have essentials sent to them tonight, and Torrian and I shall visit the prison tomorrow."

"I am coming with you." Nothing could stop her.

"Of course. Your parents shall not be deported, Siobhan," Fletcher assured her. "By this time next week, I promise you shall be reunited with them."

"How can you be so sure?" His confidence was admirable, but was it misplaced?

"My father is a duke." He exchanged a wry glance with his cousin. "A powerful duke. I've already written him and asked him to come to London. I would vow we'll be able to expose the truth and that the blighter who accused your parents bribed someone to toss them into prison. Unfortunately, it happens frequently."

At least they weren't dead.

Siobhan wouldn't tell Paddy and Kimber until Da and Maura gained their freedom.

Torrian turned toward the viscountess. "I'm sure the authorities are eager to interview you, Lady Huxley."

He angled his head toward two agents who immediately took either of her arms and removed the screaming, thrashing woman from the study.

An asylum would likely be Lady Huxley's residence rather than prison. The woman was inarguably insane.

Other agents escorted her defeated accomplices.

Desperate to put some distance between her and Fletcher before he recognized how much his actions had devasted her or before she dissolved into a weeping mess, Siobhan edged toward the door. The tumult in her mind and the maelstrom of her emotions made it almost impossible to think clearly.

And on top of tonight's event, she'd learned Da and Maura were in that foul hell-hole.

It was more than she could bear.

She must get away—must sort through this mess.

Must determine what to do next.

Staying at *De la Chance* was out of the question now.

Loving him as she did, Siobhan couldn't be around Fletcher every day. The pain would drive *her* mad. Though he wouldn't likely see it as such, his betrayal proved as excruciating as if he'd driven a rusty, serrated blade into her heart.

At least reuniting with Da and Maura would avert destitution.

In truth, Siobhan was as angry with herself as Fletcher.

She'd allowed her defenses down, and this was what came of that stupidity.

Fool. Fool. Fool.

Never again.

She had learned her lesson well.

"Huxley?" Fletcher gingerly fingered his jaw.

"Singing like a canary." Torrian Westbrook grinned. "I think we can safely assume the instigators behind the harassment have finally been apprehended."

Fletcher finally noticed her gradual retreat.

"Siobhan? Where are you going?"

She jutted her chin upward. "To my sister and brother. Where do you think?"

"They aren't in the club. Nor are any staff that weren't essential to this mission." He stepped toward her but paused, confusion whisking across his face when she glared at him. "I had the children removed to a safe location until this was over. Darius is with them. Surely, you know I wouldn't put them at risk."

But he'd put *her* in danger?

Led her to believe he had been beaten and might die?

Allowed a madwoman to point a gun at her?

She snorted.

"Do I?" She refused to meet the eyes of the men, including his cousin, after giving her a compassionate look as they quietly exited, leaving her and Fletcher alone. "I don't know you at all, Fletcher Westbrook."

Then, before she burst into tears, she fled the office.

FOURTEEN

QUARTER OF MIDNIGHT ~ THAT SAME NIGHT

Hair still damp after bathing and tending his battered face, Fletcher approached Siobhan's chamber. Eager to speak with her, he only wore trousers, an untucked shirt, and the house shoes he'd slipped on at the last minute.

A golden glow beneath her door revealed she hadn't yet gone to bed.

A self-deprecating smile bent his mouth upward.

His nightly rounds through his club might've also included passing hers and the children's chambers. To reassure himself all was well with them. Thus, he'd learned her habits.

She didn't sleep with a lamp lit. Probably a luxury her family couldn't afford.

His efficient staff reported that Siobhan had seen her siblings settled into bed after a cup of hot chocolate. She'd bathed but refused the tray he'd asked Mrs. Dough to prepare for her.

Siobhan's anger wasn't unexpected.

After all, her spirit was much of what Fletcher admired about her.

In truth, he'd anticipated her fury but had gambled that she would eventually forgive him.

He might've lost that wager, and it gutted him that he'd hurt her.

The devastation she'd tried to hide in his study earlier tonight lashed him like a saber.

Fletcher also hadn't counted on her whispering that she hadn't told him how she felt about him or Lady Huxley proclaiming Siobhan loved him. Already prepared to give his life to protect her, everything had shifted after that.

He'd become determined to live, to confess his love for her too.

In the ensuing days since discovering she was a woman, though he'd fought it with every bit of integrity and common sense, he'd done the untenable and fallen in love with his Irish lass. Sensing she wasn't ready for his declaration and hadn't come to trust Fletcher yet, he'd determined to bide his time.

However, tonight changed everything.

Looking down the barrel of a gun swiftly convinced him that life was too short to dawdle when it came to matters of the heart. He must tell her his feelings and convince her he'd kept the truth from her to protect her.

The latter would be far more difficult to do.

Tonight was no longer about apprehending the viscountess and her mealy-mouthed wimp of a husband who had been all too willing to toss his maniacal wife under the proverbial carriage if it meant a less severe penalty for him. No, this night had become about forging a future with the most remarkable, delightful, and magnificent woman Fletcher had ever met.

Having stopped praying when he left the medical profession, he paused outside her door and bowed his head.

I don't deserve it, but I need your help, Lord. Please give me the words to say.

If his brothers could see him now, they'd howl in mirth.

Holding his breath, he rapped once.

"Siobhan? I need to speak with you."

Rustling on the other side suggested she'd risen from bed or perhaps an armchair.

"Why?" Her distrustful voice filtered through the walnut door.

He leaned his forehead against the cool wood. "Because I hurt you, which was the last thing I intended to do."

"Did you set the fire too?" The wood muffled her words but not the accusation behind them.

He sighed. She might as well know everything. "Yes. I had my men stage a fire in the building next door in a fireproof container so it would not spread, and it was my man who announced it in the club. All the hullabaloo outside was also fabricated. Armond Chambeau, my theater director, recruited actors and actresses. Chandler convinced the viscountess the plan was his idea."

He'd staged the entire thing to entrap the Huxleys—specifically Lady Huxley.

Siobhan's voice, a mere thread of sound, penetrated the thick door. "We might've been shot, Fletcher. Did you not consider that?"

A hint of her earlier ire raised the pitch of her voice.

Wincing, he laid his palm flat against the door.

He'd done this to her. Made her fear for her life and his—likely her brother's and sister's too.

"Chandler removed the ball from Lady Huxley's pistol. Only he had a loaded gun."

A long pause ensued.

"Siobhan?"

"It seems you thought of everything." Sadness and resignation laced her low tone. "I'm happy you were able to catch Lady Huxley. What made you suspect her?"

"She was receptive to Chandler's complaints about me. That is why we decided on the course of action you witnessed tonight, although I still wrongly believed Lord Huxley was behind everything until a few days ago."

"That is what Chandler wanted to discuss with you privately that day I fainted, isn't it?"

"It was." Fletcher smoothed his fingers across the wood, wishing it was her he comforted. "Open the door, sweetheart. Please."

Silence reigned for several heartbeats.

"Why?"

Because I love you. I want to take you into my arms and assure you you'll never have to be afraid again. I long to taste your lips in a soul-searing kiss. To convince you that you are the most precious thing in the world to me.

Instead, he whispered, emotion clogging his throat. "Because I desperately want to see your beautiful face and to apologize for not including you. It was stupid of me."

Several more gut-wrenching moments passed before the key scratched into the lock.

However, Siobhan didn't open the door.

Taking a deep breath, Fletcher pressed the latch down, and the panel swung open.

His entire future rested upon what happened in the next few minutes.

She'd retreated to the window, her virginal nightgown enshrouding her like an angel, her ebony hair falling past her shoulders. She glanced at the bedside clock.

"It's almost midnight, Fletcher. Say what you need to say, and let me seek my bed. I'm exhausted."

Her blue eyes round and wounded, she regarded him as an injured doe would have done, leery and ready to flee.

"I'm sorry, my love. So very sorry." He held out a hand in entreaty. "I can bear anything, punishment or pain, except knowing I've hurt you. I thought it was for the best, but now I know I should have told you everything."

Twisting the gown's fabric with her fingers, she bit her lower lip and averted her gaze. Not, however, before Fletcher saw tears pooling in her incredible eyes.

He spread his arms.

"Can you forgive me, Siobhan? Please?"

With a small cry, she flew into his arms. She wrapped her arms around his neck and clung to him as if her very life depended upon it, her small breasts burning dual holes in his chest. Honeysuckle and jasmine wafted from her freshly washed skin.

Fletcher's soul took to wing in exaltation, singing with joy that this tiny woman with her big heart could forgive his foolhardiness and inconsideration.

"I was so afraid," she whispered into his neck. "Not for myself, but for you. Paddy. Kimber."

"I know, my darling." He kissed her crown, inhaling her intoxicating warmth and essence. "I vow I shall never keep another secret from you as long as I live."

She leaned back, searching his face. "That's an awful long time."

"Hopefully, several decades." Grinning, he slid his fingers into that silky mane of midnight hair that had entranced him for so long. "I suppose you shall have to marry me to ensure I keep my word."

Moisture glistened in her eyes.

"Do you love me, Fletcher?"

"More than life itself. More than I ever conceived was possible to love another person. I want you to be the first thing I see when I open my eyes in the morning and the last thing when I fall asleep. I want to experience all that life offers with you, Paddy, and Kimber." He winked and patted her delectable bottom. "And our children, of course. Lots of them."

"I love you too."

A brilliant smile blossomed on her face, humbling him that she could love him, a scoundrel and a rake.

Somewhere in the club, a clock tolled midnight.

Siobhan pulled his head downward and lifted her chin. "Kiss me."

The world stood still as he explored her mouth and

swept his hands over her gentle curves. When at last he lifted his head, she stared up at him, lips plump and red.

"I think we should marry straight away," she said breathlessly.

"Now *that* is a grand plan."

EPILOGUE

De la Chance's private salon

A FORTNIGHT LATER

With a hand on her new husband's arm, Siobhan fairly floated on air. All Fletcher's immediate family had come to London for their simple wedding except for Leonidas and Primrose, still on their honeymoon. His cousins Torrian and Cortland Marlow-Westbrook and Cortland's family also attended.

Never could she have dreamed when her family moved to London, and she'd been forced to impersonate a boy that she'd become Mrs. Fletcher Westbrook. Nor could she have imagined the warm welcome to the large family that she'd received.

Most surprising was the Duke and Duchess of Latham's genuine cordiality which they had extended toward her since their timely arrival in London nearly two weeks ago. Neither of their graces seemed the least concerned that their son had married an Irish commoner. But then, their other daughters-in-law were Spanish, French, and Scottish.

The Westbrooks seemed to enjoy turning society on its head with their unique brides.

Both Huxleys currently resided in Newgate Prison. Lord Huxley had believed he'd fare better than his lunatic wife by turning on her, but his hands were too soiled to walk free. Lady Huxley probably ought to have been committed to an insane asylum, but such things took time, and in the meanwhile, she been placed where all attempted murderesses warranted.

Fletcher had petitioned the courts to have the undesirable pair sentenced to a penal colony in Australia for life rather than hang for their offenses. He'd come by the idea after learning of her parents' unjust sentence.

Only time would tell whether his plea for mercy would be honored.

Siobhan wasn't certain she'd have been able to extend such benevolence.

Across the crowded room, Rémi and Nathalia Lemieux, Aurelie, Marchioness of Edenhaven's niece and nephew, played marbles with Paddy and Kimber.

True to his word, Fletcher had managed to free Da and Maura from Newgate. He'd offered Da a position too. Da was now the head of security at *Ivories and Aces*. He, Maura, and the children occupied a suite at *De la Chance* for now.

Thin, but their faces beaming with pride, Da and Maura stood to the side, slightly overwhelmed at the grandeur and the presence of so many nobles. Cormac O'Doherty, the villain who'd had them arrested in London, had also framed Da in Ireland for murder after losing a dice game, which is why the family had fled.

A servant approached with a tray of champagne.

Fletcher selected two flutes.

Clearing his throat, he raised his glass. "I wish to propose a toast."

Around the room, their family and friends also accepted champagne from the servants and faced him expectantly.

"To my wife. The most exceptional and courageous woman I have ever met. I am humbled she'd take a reformed rake like myself as her husband. To Siobhan. To happy ever after."

"Here, here."

"To Siobhan."

"To happy ever after."

Taking a sip, Siobhan blinked rapidly to dispel the tears pooling in her eyes. She didn't miss the intimate looks between Fletcher's parents or his married siblings and their spouses. The Westbrooks weren't the least bashful about expressing their love.

Siobhan rather liked that.

"'Tis I who is blessed." She met his amorous gaze and blushed. "You shouldn't stare at me like that."

"Like what?" If anything, Fletcher's smile became impossibly more smoldering.

Little tremors of excitement skittered up her spine and sent butterflies fluttering in her belly. "As if you'd like to gobble me like a piece of barmbrack."

Winking, he bent near her ear. "I have no idea what barmbrack is, but I definitely want to gobble you up."

Then the daring devil nipped her earlobe, causing all her bones to turn to pudding.

Good Lord, on Sunday.

Siobhan clutched his arm to stay upright.

"What say you, Mrs. Westbrook, if we leave the celebration early?"

Fletcher waggled his eyebrows.

She brushed a kiss across his firm mouth, gratified to see sparks ignite in his green eyes. Two could play at this game of seduction.

"I'd say, what are you waiting for, Mr. Westbrook?"

Hand in hand, Siobhan and Fletcher ran from the parlor, the laughter and hoots from their families following them down the corridor. At the foot of the stairs, Fletcher swept her into his arms.

"I love you, Fletcher." She cupped his cheek, and he pressed his face into her palm as he effortlessly carried her up the stairway.

"Not nearly as much as I love you, my darling Irish lass, and I intend to spend a lifetime proving it."

Looping her arms around his neck, Siobhan nipped his earlobe, curving her mouth into a gratified smile when he groaned.

"Minx."

"I learned that from you, husband."

They'd reached her chamber, and still holding her in his arms, he opened the door. "I cannot wait to teach you much more."

"Neither can I."

I hope you enjoyed
KISS A RAKE AT MIDNIGHT
and following the romantic journey
of Fletcher and Siobhan

*If you'd like to leave a review please
scan the following QR Code.*

SCAN HERE TO LEAVE A REVIEW FOR
"KISS A RAKE AT MIDNIGHT"

*Keep reading for a FREE PREVIEW of
UNMASKED AT MIDNIGHT,
Book 8
Chronicles of the Westbrook Brides Series...*

FROM THE DESK OF COLLETTE CAMERON®

Fletcher Westbrook had me puzzled for the first few books in the series. I knew what motivated him and what he most feared, but I didn't know who his perfect heroine would be until I wrote Sean/Siobhan into ***MINUET AT MIDNIGHT***. I instantly knew she should be his soulmate. They are opposites in so many ways, but opposites do attract.

Though it's not an uncommon trope, Siobhan is my first heroine to pretend to be a man. Life for women without means or family was difficult in times gone by, and desperation frequently forced women into prostitution.

I mentioned a few ice flavors Gunter's Tea Shop served. The ices were very similar to modern-day ice cream, except we wouldn't consider many flavors popular then for our sweet treats now. I don't think I'd enjoy a parmesan ice.

Hugs,
Collette Cameron®

Unmasked AT Midnight

USA Today Bestselling Author

COLLETTE CAMERON

FREE PREVIEW

Woodhaven, Cumberland, England

APRIL 1828 ~ MID-MORNING

There she is—the woman I mean to court.

Lord Darius Westbrook took in Eudora Clarke's loveliness. Her beauty—silky brunette hair, creamy ivory skin, an oval face, rosebud pink lips, and a petite but superbly rounded figure—filled him with awe, even from across the street.

Peeking from beneath a feathered bonnet, her soft doe-like eyes framed by lush sable lashes, Eudora gave Darius a demure smile. Her mother, Mrs. Gertrude Clarke, narrowed her sharp gaze on him, her features hardening into severe lines in her rather mannish face as she said something to her daughter.

It confounded him how a woman as plain and unremarkable as a sheet of foolscap and with a figure resembling a lumpy cotton bale could have produced such a beauty. Only the Good Lord knew the answer to that mystery. Still, as dour and unapproachable as Mrs. Clarke was, no one could fault her diligence in chaperoning her only offspring.

Eudora dutifully averted her gaze, but not before her smile widened a fraction in rebellious flirtation.

To Darius's utter delight, the delectable Miss Clarke wasn't quite as biddable as she appeared and as, no doubt, her formidable mother preferred.

He wasn't the least deterred by Mrs. Clarke's disapproval.

A prize easily won was no prize at all. The pursuit, overcoming obstacles, and emerging victorious made the quest all that much more worthwhile. Darius would win over Mrs. Clarke and court Eudora.

Of that, he had no doubt.

Enough woolgathering. Back to work.

He studied the sign he'd just hung outside his establishment with a critical eye before touching one side ever-so-slightly to bring the slat into perfect balance. His twin, Cassius, had painted the beveled rectangle, flawlessly capturing the establishment's welcoming atmosphere.

A musical giggle drew Darius's attention to the delightful feminine bundle swathed in lavender and pink across the cobbled village square.

Eudora was the essence of womanliness.

And yet, a question continued to niggle in his mind; would his mother and sister like her?

An octagon fountain burbled happily in the spring sunshine as a pair of round-cheeked urchins—amid squeals of delight—floated their sailboats in the makeshift sea. Men lifted their hats and dipped their chins as Eudora and her imposing mother meandered along, stopping to peruse the window displays.

Glowing, Eudora glided from shop to shop.

Mrs. Clarke glowered and lumbered in her daughter's wake.

Darius waited for the ping of jealousy his rivals' attention should warrant, but nothing so unpleasant disturbed the morning's serenity. Likely because of his confidence that Eudora returned his regard. Surely she must. Else, why would she seek his company despite her mother's censure?

A year ago, the mere thought of courting a woman would've sent him hightailing it to the farthest corners of the earth. But then, a year ago, he'd still held a commission in His Majesty's Navy and wasn't the proud owner of Westbrook's Book & Coffee Emporium, his bookstore and coffeehouse.

Excitement and anxiousness battled for dominance when he thought of the week-long grand opening in just two months.

He'd invited several authors for the event, including his brother Leonidas. His mother had suggested the authors come masked on the final evening to add intrigue and to see if the guests could guess who they were. Mother, who had planned too many grand events to count, insisted the finale include refreshments and a string quartet. Darius didn't mind the former, but the latter seemed more conducive to a Society ball.

Nevertheless, he conceded to her recommendations.

After all, the duchess was a force to be reckoned with and her organizational expertise was legendary.

Invitations to the more prestigious guests had gone out weeks ago, while a sign in the window invited the locals to participate in the daily activities as well. Naturally, the Westbrook brood, including Grandmama, and his parents, the Duke and Duchess of Latham, would be in attendance.

Westbrook's Book & Coffee Emporium welcomed everyone, especially the vivacious and breathtakingly lovely Eudora Clarke. Although of marriageable age, Eudora exuded a girlish charm. Her bubbly temperament and winsome smile had captivated him from the first day he'd met her at Saint Andrew's Church.

So immersed in his thoughts about Eudora, Darius

tottered unsteadily when the sturdy ladder he stood upon teetered.

What the…?

Jostled from his romantic musings, he glanced down, unsurprised to see his twin grinning up at him.

He countered his brother's grin with a glower.

"You're gaping at her like a moonstruck swain, Dare."

Cassius didn't appear the least contrite for almost toppling Darius off the ladder.

Ignoring his brother's teasing, Darius descended a couple of rungs and, with great satisfaction, examined the store's bay window. The display needed a few more books and other reading-related doodads before he would consider it completed, but it was coming along quite nicely.

Satisfaction burgeoned behind his breastbone. Compelled by grit and determination, *he* had done this, not his father's wealth and influence.

His twin continued to grin like a drunken buffoon.

"I'm grateful you delivered the sign in person, but shouldn't you return to your art studio in Brighton, Cass?"

"No." Cassius shook his head. "No, I don't believe I shall."

Darius tamped down a surge of annoyance. "I'm sure you have eager patrons vying to have their portraits painted."

There was a time Darius worried his twin would never paint again.

"My patrons can wait. Besides, you know I always bring my supplies with me. I might even dabble at a landscape or two while I'm here." Cassius leaned a shoulder against the doorframe. Deep blue eyes, so like Darius's, glinted with suppressed worry as he rubbed his chin. "In truth, I determined just this morning that as a good brother, I ought to remain and lend a hand. Perhaps I'll stay for a few weeks. I might even recruit Layton to assist."

Bollocks.

Betrayal and cynicism had skewed their half-brother Layton's view on marriage and on life in general. The taciturn eldest Westbrook sibling was the last person Darius wanted advice from.

"*Lend a hand*?" Darius released a snort worthy of a Royal Ascot racehorse. "Spying on my courtship of Miss Clarke, you mean."

"Guilty." Cassius burst into laughter. "It's my duty as your twin. We've already had multiple siblings charge headlong to the altar with undue haste. I'm here to assure you don't make the same mistake. Did you forget our vow of bachelorhood?"

A young man's immature declaration.

Cassius had been scorned in love, as had Layton. Naturally, neither brother had an interest in marriage.

"Courting her is not a proposal, Cass," Darius said

dryly. He might very well find they weren't as compatible as he hoped. If he fell in love, he wouldn't mind a quick union either.

Besides, was it truly a mistake to marry for love, even if Society deemed the wooing rushed? Despite their relatively short courtships and improbable matches, his siblings, Leonidas, Althelia, Adolphus, Lucius, and Fletcher, were all ridiculously happy.

Darius supposed he would have to wait and see how his courting progressed. Easier done without an interfering twin hanging about or a brooding older brother who had as much use for marriage as he did carbuncles.

Darius had chosen Woodhaven as the location for his establishment as much because of the quaint but growing township's charm as the proximity to his father's ducal estate—a mere forty-five-minute carriage ride away.

Convenient, but perhaps too much so.

In the past week alone, Mother and Father had come unannounced thrice to check on the bookstore's progress.

Or, more aptly, to see if their second youngest child's foray into the world of commerce required financial assistance—which it did not. Despite his rather meager naval compensation, Darius had saved enough capital to invest in the venture, thanks to adhering to a frugal budget, along with investments from his writer-brother Leonidas and his half-brother Fletcher, who owned two successful social clubs.

The only ripple was how Darius would support a wife—*if* he decided to propose—in the manner she was accustomed to until the bookstore became solvent. He didn't mind economizing—it taught a person discipline and prudence, and also built character. However, as certain as he was that red blood pumped through his veins, he was equally convinced that Eudora would not appreciate frugality.

Taking a deep breath of the refreshing sea air, he shoved that disconcerting truth to a corner of his mind to examine later.

Love conquers all.

Was he in love with the fetching miss?

Something very pleasant burbled behind his ribs and warmed his blood. Surely that was love or something very near the emotion.

Darius Ethan Trent Westbrook, you are in suds up to your starched neckcloth.

Yes. Yes. I am.

And he couldn't summon a jot of concern about his newfound infatuation.

As if sensing Darius's ruminations, Mrs. Clarke glanced over her sturdy shoulder. Her squarish features granite hard, she gave him a scorching *you-better-not-be-having-impure-thoughts-about-my-daughter* glare.

Rather than give her a cocky salute and an unrepentant grin, as had been his first instinct, he dipped his chin deferentially. No point in adding fodder to the blaze he wanted to extinguish.

"The dragon is breathing fire today, I see." Echoing Darius's thoughts, his twin veered his gaze toward the Clarkes.

An unapologetic social climber, Mrs. Clarke was a fearsome foe. Darius had determined that truth from their very first meeting and the ensuing stilted conversations. Eudora, on the other hand, didn't seem as concerned with social standing as her mother.

Despite his father's title and his family's powerful influence in Society, as a younger son, Darius was clearly low on the matron's list of appropriate suitors. Nevertheless, he suspected, Eudora typically got exactly what she wanted.

Darius just needed to ensure she picked him.

Her mother would most likely come around.

After all, didn't all parents desire their children's happiness above all else?

His parents always had.

A horrific thought invaded his mind, bringing his romantic musings to a grinding halt.

Would Eudora expect her mother to live with them?

Ye gods.

No force on earth would compel Darius to share a domicile with that she-dragon. He expelled a deep breath.

He'd have to cross that bridge when he came to it. And right now, that bridge was some distance away.

"She's just a protective mother," Darius said, hoping to convince himself. "With a daughter so lovely, she has to be."

"If you say so." Cassius's tone conveyed he didn't believe that to be the case. "I think she just doesn't like you. You're not inheriting a peerage, nor are you wealthy."

"Thank you for pointing out those deficiencies, brother," Darius drawled, his tone dryer than hearth ash. Though, in truth, Darius didn't consider his lack of a peerage title a detriment, nor was he a bloody pauper.

"I know you are infatuated, Darius, and I shall not besmirch Miss Clarke's character, but she's not the sweet, biddable miss she pretends." Genuine concern and affection softened his twin's features. "I've already discerned that from the short time I've been here. You are blind to her faults. Trust me when I tell you my ears are burning from the tales I've been told. I fear you are dashing headlong into a tempest."

"You would have me listen to gossip too?" Darius snorted, betrayal rooting around his belly. "You could at least pretend to like her for my sake."

Cassius shrugged. "I shan't dish out platitudes to soothe your ego."

"When have you ever?" Darius snapped.

"Exactly so, and that is how you prefer it. And not

that you need reminding because I know how intelligent you are, but the truth is still the truth, even if you refuse to believe it." His expression somber, Cassius disappeared inside the bookstore.

Why did the rotter have to be right?

Head bowed, Darius sighed.

Was he running headlong into a storm?

Having several older brothers in line for the duchy ahead of him might have much to do with Mrs. Clarke's disapproval. Or mayhap it was that Darius had determined to pursue his passion and open a bookstore and coffeehouse and therefore would smell of the shop.

Eudora's tinkling laugh drew his attention. She shook her head at something her mother had said, causing her parasol's pink fringe to jiggle. A seaborne breeze had the temerity to tease a glossy curl near her cheek, and Darius heaved another deep sigh.

Yes, he could be quite content in Woodhaven.

But would it be with her?

He took another step down the ladder.

A series of outraged, muffled *honks* interrupted his admittedly moon-eyed regard of the delectable Miss Clarke.

Hunched over and wearing a gown in an indeterminable shade of brown—or was it drab-green?—a slender young woman bore down upon him. Her rapt attention remained riveted on a fat goose waddling ahead of her.

"Sir Waddlesby!" she huffed, grabbing for him and missing. "You are in so much trouble."

Sir... Waddlesby?

Oh, she meant the goose.

An embroidered cobalt blue band encircled the goose's neck, and he clasped a cherry-red glove firmly in his beak.

Darius had no idea that geese could run so fast.

The gander's speed was impressive.

Honk-honk. Honk-honk.

Passersby stopped, laughed, and pointed as the woman chased the naughty wing-flapping fowl.

"Sir Waddlesby. Stop this instant. That is not your glove," she panted as she pelted along, the goose remaining just out of her reach. "It's Mrs. Tenney's, and if you ruin it..."

Just as Darius stepped onto the last rung, Sir Waddlesby spied the ladder and dove between its wooden legs.

If a goose could grin in triumph, that dratted creature did.

The recalcitrant goose's pursuer realized too late what her ill-mannered pet had done. She tried to stop but barreled full-on into the ladder. In a tangle of limbs, ladder rungs, and feathers, Darius landed atop the woman with a resounding thud.

I hope you enjoyed this FREE PREVIEW of
Unmasked at Midnight
Book 8
Chronicles of the Westbrook Brides Series.

You can currently read it as part of the
Gentlemen and Gloves
Lords and Ladies of St. James Book 5
— *a multi-author anthology.*
If you'd like to keep reading please scan the following QR Code.

SCAN HERE TO GET "UNMASKED AT MIDNIGHT"

GIGGLES ARE GUARANTEED
COLLETTE'S CHERIS READER GROUP

If you love to chat about all things romance-book related and enjoy taking part in fun and engaging live events, contests, and giveaways join **Collette's Chèris VIP Reader Group,** my exclusive private book group on Facebook.

Giggles are guaranteed!

Hope to see you there,

Collette Cameron®

Please scan the following QR Code to join:

ALSO BY COLLETTE CAMERON®
BLUE ROSE ROMANCE® LLC

COLLETTE CAMERON'S®

COMPLETE BOOK LIST

CHRONICLES OF THE WESTBROOK BRIDES

A Romantic Opposites Attract Mystery & Suspense

Family Saga Regency Romance

Moonlight Wishes and Midnight Kisses — Bonus Novella

Midnight Christmas Waltz — Book 1

Mission at Midnight — Book 2

The Midnight Marquess — Book 3

Holly, Mistletoe, and Midnight Snow — Book 4

The Wallflower's Midnight Waltz— Book 5

Minuet at Midnight— Book 6

Kiss a Rake at Midnight — Book 7

Unmasked at Midnight — Book 8

Once Upon a Midnight Dream — Book 9

Memories Made at Midnight — Book 10

DUKES COME CALLING

A Sensual Marriage of Convenience

Regency Historical Romance

A Diamond for a Duke — Book 1

Only a Duke Would Dare — Book 2

A December with a Duke — Book 3

What Would a Duke Do? — Book 4

Wooed by a Wicked Duke — Book 5

Duchess of His Heart — Book 6

Never Dance with a Duke — Book 7

Wedding Her Christmas Duke — Book 8

The Debutante and the Duke — Book 9

Loved by a Dangerous Duke — Book 10

How to Win a Duke's Heart — Book 11

When a Duke Desires a Lass — Book 12

My Dearest Duke — Book 13

FOR THE LOVE OF AN EARL (Wicked Earls' Club)

A Humorous Aristocrat and Wallflower

Regency Romance Adventure

Earl of Wainthorpe — Book 1

Earl of Scarborough — Book 2

Earl of Keyworth — Book 3

Earl of Renshaw — Book 4

HEART OF A SCOT

A Passionate Enemies to Lovers

Scottish Highlander Historical Mystery

Romance Adventure

To Love a Highland Laird — Book 1

To Redeem a Highland Rogue — Book 2

To Seduce a Highland Scoundrel — Book 3

To Woo a Highland Warrior — Book 4

HIGHLAND HEATHER ROMANCING A SCOT: CASTLE BRIDES

A Passionate Enemies to Lovers Second Chance Scottish Highlander Mystery Romance

Wishes and Wonder — Book 9

A Yuletide Highlander — Book 10

SECRETS OF SCANDALOUS LADIES

A Romantic Class Difference Forced Proximity

Regency Romance with Aristocrats

A Lady, A Kish, A Christmas Wish — Book 1

No Lady for the Lord — Book 2

Love Lessons for a Lady — Book 3

His One and Only Lady — Book 4

Never a Proper Lady — Book 5

Lady Tempts a Rogue — Book 6

THE CULPEPPER MISSES

A Humorous Wallflower Family Saga

Regency Romantic Comedy

The Earl and the Spinster — Book 1

The Marquis and the Vixen — Book 2

The Lord and the Wallflower — Book 3

The Buccaneer and the Bluestocking — Book 4

The Lieutenant and the Lady — Book 5

THE HONORABLE ROGUES®
A Second Chance Redeemable Rogue
and Wallflower Regency Romance

A Kiss for a Rogue — Book 1

A Bride for a Rogue — Book 2

A Rogue's Scandalous Wish — Book 3

To Capture a Rogue's Heart — Book 4

The Rogue and the Wallflower — Book 5

A Rose for a Rogue — Book 6

'Twas the Rogue Before Christmas — Book 7

A Rogue Worth the Risk — Book 8

ABOUT THE AUTHOR

COLLETTE CAMERON®

USA Today Bestselling author Collette Cameron® is renowned for her captivating, humorous, and heart-warming Scottish and Regency historical romance novels. With over 65 published titles, over 1.4 million books sold around the world, and multiple writing awards to her credit, Collette is a well-known author in the world of historical romance. Readers love her witty and relatable characters including daring rogues, dashing scoundrels, and the strong and spirited heroines who capture their hearts. From the rugged highlands to the refined drawing rooms of Regency England, Collette's novels will transport you to another time and place, where love and adventure are just a page away.

Collette's Sweet-to-Spicy Timeless Romances® are the perfect escape for readers looking for romantic escape, poignant inspiration, engaging humor, and entertaining stories.

Based in the Pacific Northwest, Collette is surrounded by the lush greenery and rainy skies that inspire her writing. She dreams of one day splitting her time between the Pacific Northwest and Scotland. In the meantime, she indulges in her love of all things cobalt blue, dachshunds, chocolate, and of course, crafting her next historical romance.

Blue Rose Romance® LLC
PO Box 167
Scappoose, Oregon 97056 USA
collettecameron.com

If you haven't joined Collette's exclusive mailing list scan the folloing QR Code to sign up!
You'll get access to exclusive content, sneak peeks, contests, giveaways, and more...
(P.S. No spammy stuff.)

Follow Collette on social media.
Scan the following QR Code: